Priscilla Anne Westmorland, Rose Sophia Weigall

The Letters of Lady Burghersh

afterwards Countess of Westmorland - from Germany and France during the

campaign of 1813-14

Priscilla Anne Westmorland, Rose Sophia Weigall

The Letters of Lady Burghersh
afterwards Countess of Westmorland - from Germany and France during the campaign of 1813-14

ISBN/EAN: 9783337734978

Printed in Europe, USA, Canada, Australia, Japan

Cover: Foto ©Andreas Hilbeck / pixelio.de

More available books at **www.hansebooks.com**

THE LETTERS

OF

LADY BURGHERSH

(AFTERWARDS COUNTESS OF WESTMORLAND)

FROM GERMANY AND FRANCE DURING
THE CAMPAIGN OF 1813-14

EDITED BY HER DAUGHTER

LADY ROSE WEIGALL

WITH PORTRAITS

LONDON
JOHN MURRAY, ALBEMARLE STREET
1893

PREFACE

I HAVE been asked several times to allow this collection of my mother's early letters from abroad to be printed. I have hesitated about doing so, knowing how averse she was to the indiscriminate publication of private papers. But now that the events to which these letters allude have all passed into the domain of history this objection no longer holds good, and those friends of her later years who still survive may be glad of this remembrance of her. A wider public may perhaps appreciate this contemporary sketch of a great episode of history.

The campaign to which these letters

relate was that of 1813. In that year the whole of Europe was in arms against Napoleon. While the English under Wellington were fighting his armies in Spain, the Russian, Austrian, and Prussian Governments were united for the purpose of driving him and the remnants of his 'Grand Army' (then retreating from Russia) out of Germany.

There had been abortive peace negotiations at Prague, in which the diplomatists of all the Governments concerned had taken part, so that nearly all the foremost men in Europe were gathered together at the Allied Sovereigns' headquarters.

Amongst the English there were Lord Aberdeen, Sir Charles Stewart, and others, all of whom were well known to Lady Burghersh. She had had the advantage of living from her earliest childhood among wide interests, and in a brilliant political

society. Her father, as well as his celebrated brothers, was constantly in high
office, and his house was one of the meeting places of the official people of the day.
Many foreigners—especially many of the
French *émigrés*—were also amongst the
frequenters of the house. A very careful education had developed her natural
abilities and fitted her to appreciate these
advantages more than many young girls
might have done, and when she first went
abroad, young as she was, she had the
habit of society, a perfect knowledge of
French and Italian, and a good general
idea of the leading questions of the day.
She used, however, in later days to say
she regretted that her youth and inexperience at the time of the campaign had led
her into rash and hasty judgments, and
had prevented her deriving as much real
benefit from all she saw and heard as

she might have done had she been older.

France had at that time been absolutely closed to England during the twenty years the war had lasted (with the exception of the short period of the Peace of Amiens in 1802), and everything in France was therefore absolutely new and strange to the younger generation of English people at this date. The horror and dread of the name of ' Bonaparte ' was at its height in England, and no doubt intensified in the society Lady Burghersh lived in by their association with the Bourbons and others of the French noblesse, who lived in much intimacy, during their years of exile, with all the Wellesley family and their relations.

CONTENTS

—◦◦◦—

LETTER I.

LETTER II.

LETTER III.

LETTER IV.

LETTER X.

LETTER XI.

LETTER XII.

LETTER XIII.

LETTER XVIII.

LETTER XIX.

LETTER XX.

LETTER XXI.

LETTER XXII.

LETTER XXVII.

LETTER XXVIII.

LETTER XXIX.

LETTER XXX.

a

LETTER XLII.

LETTER XLIII.

JOURNAL

OF

LADY BURGHERSH

———◦———

PRISCILLA ANN WELLESLEY POLE, born in March 1793, was the youngest daughter of William Wellesley Pole (afterwards Lord Maryborough), the second son of the Earl of Mornington, of musical celebrity, and brother to the Duke of Wellington and Marquis Wellesley. Her mother was a daughter of Admiral Forbes.

At the age of eighteen she married Lord Burghersh, who had been aide-de-camp to her uncle (then Sir Arthur Wellesley) in the Peninsula. About two years after their marriage an appointment was offered to Lord Burghersh to go out

B

as Commissioner (or, as it would now be called, 'military attaché') to the head-quarters of the Austrian Army in Germany, where the 'allied sovereigns' (the Emperors of Russia and Austria and the King of Prussia) were in the field against Napoleon and his army, then retreating from Russia.

The appointment, though flattering, was not welcome to either of them. For many reasons Lord Burghersh would have preferred to remain with his regiment, and he was aware that his selection would cause jealousies and ill-will on the part of some, then on the spot, with whom he had no wish to enter into competition. But the Government had chosen him, and he had no alternative but to carry out his orders with a soldier's unquestioning obedience.

At this time the difficulty of getting from England to Germany was not small, for all the French and Dutch ports were closed against English ships, and it was necessary to undertake a long sea voyage (with the chances of falling into the hands of French cruisers) before a port at which to land could be reached.

For a short time Hamburg was open, and Lord Burghersh hoped to land there, but before he was ready to start Hamburg fell again into the hands of the French, and then the only way left to get from England to North Germany was to go by sea to Gothenburg, in Sweden; thence across Sweden to Ystad, and there re-embark and cross the Baltic to Stralsund, on the coast of Prussia.

The season of the year was getting late, and the prospects of the journey and subsequent winter campaign full of hard-ships and difficulties; but the young wife was not frightened, and determined to face them all with her husband, though all her family, and especially her father, tried strongly to dissuade her. She had never been strong, was quite unused to travelling, and, though she had been married two years, was only twenty years old, so that there was much to be said for her father's strong objections to her undertaking such a journey in the face of her youth, her inexperience, and her delicate health.   But her husband wished to have her with him, and her mother then said, that being so, and she having no children or duties requiring her presence at home, it was right she should go ; and so it was settled.   A great many preparations had to be made for so long and, under the circumstances, so adventurous a journey.   One difficulty was as to the servants to be taken.   Ordinary servants, accustomed merely to the usual routine of a London life, would, they felt, be worse than useless.   This was especially the case with the young lady's maid.   It was absolutely necessary to have in her place some older woman, who would be more of a nurse and protector to her young mistress ; but the difficulty was to find anyone willing to face such an expedition.

At last an elderly Frenchwoman, named Madame Legoux, who had been befriended by her mother, and had known her from a child, volunteered to go. She proved a most devoted and excellent servant, and was invaluable through all the difficulties of the subsequent winter. They also took with them men-servants and horses. A private secretary also accompanied them.

As has been said, it was not safe then for single vessels to attempt the passage through the French fleet in the North Sea, so their departure was delayed till a convoy carrying subsidies to the German Government was ready to sail, and they finally embarked at Yarmouth in one of the vessels escorting this convoy in September 1813, but were driven back and delayed ten days by contrary winds before they finally got off. The passage was rough and slow, and lasted eleven days. On October 10 they landed on the Swedish coast, and Lady Burghersh's first letter from abroad is addressed to her sister Emily, and dated from

Gottenburgh : October 11, 1813

My dearest E.,—I am so lucky as to find a messenger here who sets off for England, so I hasten to give you an account of all I have done since yesterday. I was but just in time to send off my letter to Mama by the packet. The moment I had done writing it (about twelve o'clock) we left the frigate and got into the boat ; but as we had eight or nine miles to row from Wingo Sound to Gottenburgh, we were advised to land at a place called Warholm, in Wingo Sound. It is, in fact, only a few scattered wooden houses, built here and there among the barren rocks which compose the whole coast of Sweden as far as I have yet seen. Upon landing there we found no post-

house, so we went into one of the houses
and by luck found a man who could understand a little English and German. By
his directions we walked on about half a
mile to another house, where another man,
who also understood a little English, prepared to get us conveyances to carry us
to Gottenburgh, a distance of about seven
miles all through these bare rocks. You
can't conceive how dreary and miserable
it looks; as far as the eye can reach,
nothing but these rocks—not a tree, but
only here and there between the rocks
a little patch of ground to feed a cow and
grow turnips.

While they were preparing the vehicles
we stayed in the house, a very poor place,
but very clean, and the people so very
intelligent that you can make them understand almost anything by signs. The
language is the softest and prettiest thing

I ever heard. The men are remarkably good-looking, but the women and children sodden, owing, I suppose, to the heat of the stoves. Their rooms are all strewed with bits of yew, and from the ceiling they hang their provision of cakes for the year. They only bake them twice a year. The cakes are as hard as stone, but very good. I ate some last night.

After waiting in the cottage a long time, the vehicles arrived. They consisted of little open carts, so small that it is difficult for two people to sit, with no springs, and drawn each by one horse. Into two of these we got—B. and I into one, the messenger and Madame Legoux into another—and the rest of the household, A.D.C. and all, we were obliged to leave in the ship to come ashore to-day with the carriage, &c. We proceeded in these along the road, which is cut through

the rocks, jolted, as you may suppose,
most terribly, and at the end of seven
miles arrived at a ferry, where we got
into a boat, and, having crossed, found
ourselves in the *faubourg* of Gottenburgh.
We were then obliged to have recourse
to our legs alone to carry us to an inn
kept by an Englishman, which we were
told was not far off, where B. meant to
deposit me and go himself to the English
Consul's to find out where we had better
establish ourselves, &c. It was then
nearly dark, very cold, and the road so
shocking that in five minutes we were wet
up to the ankles. We were also very
hungry, having had nothing since we left
the ship but a little rum and water, the
only thing we could get in the houses at
Warholm, and which, I assure you, nasty
as it was, we were too glad to have. Instead of finding the English inn near, we

walked nearly two miles before we got to it, and then! such a place! like the worst sort of public-house. The man said his house was full; he had no beds, and only one room which he could allow us to go into, while B. and the messenger went on to the Consul's. We wished to have gone on at once, if possible, to the Consul's, but we were told it was two miles further, and therefore we could not attempt it. Into this room, therefore, we went: no fire, no stove, but we got some shoes and stockings from the women of the house, and put them on as well as we could, having seven or eight men in the room passing and repassing.

Conceive our happiness when B. returned into the room, having met the Consul's brother, Mr. Norrie, in his carriage, who immediately took us in and carried us to his house. There I was shown into a very pretty, well-furnished bedroom, where Mrs. Norrie, a young Swedish woman, was ending her toilette. I was almost starved, and she gave me some very tough cold beef, with some Swedish cake and a glass of porter, which I found delicious.

I stayed there about an hour while Mr. Norrie went out to get us lodgings—for the inns here are so horrid, he said, we could not stay there. He returned with the good news that he had got rooms for us at the house of an Englishwoman who has lived here twenty years, but still she is English. Here we immediately moved, and we are very comfortable. We got a very clean bed and the most exquisite coffee I ever tasted. All other eatables we must get from a traiteur's. There is a very remarkable and strong smell all over the country—not unpleasant,

I think, but everything you eat tastes of it, and I am not yet used to it. The cold I do not mind; it is very dry and bracing, and none of that raw, damp feel which kills one in England. I am very well, except a little stiff from the jolting of the cart yesterday.

The messenger who will carry this comes from the headquarters; the news he brings is so good that I think I shall probably (from the position of the armies) find Berlin my best headquarters. We hear the Crown Prince has crossed the Elbe, and Blücher is on the point of doing so. . . . I long to hear from England beyond what I can express! but it is a great comfort to have been able to write so soon, and to-day, at leisure. God bless you, my dearest E.

Ever yr. aff.

P. B.

Lady Burghersh to her Mother

Gottenburgh : Wednesday morning,
October 13, 1813

My dearest Mama, — We are just
setting off for Ystad ; the distance is about
250 English miles. We shall arrive about
Saturday. We are obliged to hire coach-
men here to drive all the way, as they
furnish horses but no postboys at the inns,
and we are obliged to carry with us all
the ' prog ' we want on the road ; the only
thing they furnish at the inns being coffee
and eggs (without bread). . . .

I have seen nothing more of Gottenburgh since the day I went out to get your
gloves and some furs for myself. There
is not much to see, for it is a monstrous
dull town. There are no shop windows ;
most of the shops are at the top of the

houses, so there is nothing to see ; but the quay is handsome.   I did not go out much because I have a little cold, caught, I suppose, by the wet walk we had the day we arrived.   It was very slight, but I thought it best to take care of it, as I had three days here quiet before I began my journey. I should not mention it, only I knew you would rather I told you every trifle.   I am well to-day, and the weather is mild.

I should be very glad if you would write to Grandmama,[1] for me.   She begged I would write to her as soon as I landed. I have not time ; pray tell her so, and say I will write to her from the next place where I stop.

You will perhaps wonder how my time can be so taken up, but you have no idea how much falls on my shoulders.   Dear

---

[1] Lady Mornington, the mother of the Duke of Wellington.

little Madame Legoux, who is the greatest comfort and treasure to me in all essentials, has not, of course, an idea of managing or settling anything. She says, *J'ai tant souffert que ma mémoire ne me sert plus.* I am obliged to remember and think of everything. Certainly Providence gives one capacity for what one must do, for I find really no difficulty in arranging everything, not only for myself, but for the servants too. B. has enough out-door work to do, but we do very well, and I am never the least worried about anything, owing, I believe, to having my time fully occupied, and so much the better. As to Herbert,[2] he is of about as much use as a child, and frightened to death at everything. James[3] is the best servant I ever saw, and we find young Aubin, the A.D.C., so active, intelligent, and ready

[2] Their footman.   [3] The groom.

for anything, that he is of the greatest use. What a household history! but I know they are details you will like to know.

The Emperor of Russia has made Madame Moreau a Princess, and given her 100,000 roubles a year—about 7,000*l.*, I believe.

A mail is just arrived from England— brings us papers to the 6th, but no letters, a great disappointment. I must end—the carriages are ready. God bless you all. How I long to hear of you.

Yr. most affec.

P. A. B.

Lady Burghersh to her Father

Ystad: Sunday, October 17

My dearest Papa,—We have just met two couriers landed this morning from

Stralsund on their way to England. I
seize the opportunity to write and tell you
we arrived here late last night, having left
Gottenburgh on Wednesday. The wind
is now directly against us, and the Swedish
packets cannot sail from hence unless it is
quite fair ; therefore I don't know how long
we may be kept here. We made a good
journey, and the travelling here is, I believe, as good as anywhere but England.
The horses are excessively small, but they
go at a great rate. They put four abreast
to each carriage, which are driven by the
coachman whom you hire at the beginning
of the journey, and they carry you through.
When the road is heavy they put on two
additional horses in front, with a postilion.
The harness is all rope, and you are also
obliged to buy that yourself, as they furnish
only the horses.

We sent on a courier to order the

horses for us, otherwise we should have wasted about two hours at each stage. As it was, we had often half an hour or an hour to stop while they were putting to. The inns, to be sure, are such as we have no idea of in England, but they are clean, and as we have our own beds we do very well, though we generally find but one room of a few feet square to eat, drink, and sleep in. I have never seen a carpet or curtain, basin or jug, but as soon as we arrived at our sleeping-place we sent the servants into the yard to snatch up the pans the chickens feed out of, or the pails from the stable, and made use of them.

As to eatables, we got at nearly all the inns most excellent coffee, eggs, and smoked fish (which is very good) ; that is all, except at Helsingborg, where we dined on Friday, and got some roast mutton and white bread for the first time.

Helsingborg is much the best town we passed through. It has a castle, and the view from it of Elsinore and the coast of Denmark is beautiful. The country on this side of Helsingborg is so different from that on the side of Gottenburgh that it is quite like a different region. The first two days' journey we passed through a completely barren country, nothing but rocks and sands, and here and there a very little wood. But from this to Lund and Helsingborg is very fertile, and well cultivated. The dress of the people is also quite different ; the women's dress beautiful, if any of *them* were at all so, but I have not seen yet a pretty Swedish woman.

We heard a great deal of news at every posthouse, but unfortunately it happened to be different everywhere, and the fact is they live upon reports and lies. All the people seem really interested and eager for the good cause, and Bernadotte seems very popular throughout the country. The courier who will take this letter brings an account of an alarm at Berlin from a movement of Ney's, but he seems to know little about it, and I don't suppose we shall know anything true till we get to Stralsund. I hear Sir C. Stewart has left the Prussian army to be attached to the Crown Prince. I must end, for the courier waits for this, and I must write to Mama. God bless you, my dearest Papa.

Yr. most aff.

PRISCILLA.

Lady Burghersh to her Mother

Ystad : October 17

My dearest Mama,—I have written to Papa, but you will like to hear from me that my cold is well, and that I am not the least tired, though I have been travelling every day from eight in the morning till twelve at night. I have never felt the least fatigue for a moment. The third day of my journey I found the bad food (smoked fish and brown, or rather *black*, bread) disagreed with me, so I have taken care since not to eat their food ; but when I could not get meat and bread to cook myself, contented myself with eggs and coffee, and did very well. The best dinner I have yet made was yesterday, when we stopped at a place where there was no fire, and nothing in the house but four raw eggs. The people were so savage they would not attempt lighting a fire or doing anything for us ; then our cooking machine came into use. We had the remains of two cold fowls, which we put in with some of Aubert's portable soup, some of our own vegetable powder, and some potatoes, and it was quite excellent. Madame Legoux is quite well, not the least tired, and as merry and happy as possible. We have a great deal of fun, certainly, when one has made up one's mind to face all kinds of difficulties . . . but one pleasure is the cleanliness here. God knows how we shall find it in Germany. I must put up this to give to the courier.

Lady Burghersh to her Mother

Ystad : October 18, 1813

My dearest Mama,—Having at length a little leisure, I begin to write to you in comfort, and shall continue adding to this till I go from this place, and I shall leave it to be carried by the next courier that passes.

I have been made quite happy to-day

by the arrival of English papers and letters for the first time. The latest date of the letters is the 4th, though the papers are up to the 8th, but the delight and joy of seeing your handwriting was beyond expression. . . . The wind is completely against our sailing, and the weather is so bad that I have never been outside the doors yet. We have got a gun brig to go across in, for, on going on board the packets, B. found them so horridly bad and dirty that he said it was out of the question our going in them. The captain of the brig seems to think this wind will last some days, so here we must remain.

To be sure, Yarmouth, which we complained of, was paradise compared to this place, yet we find ourselves quite comfortable here, by comparison with the other inns we have been in, and the living here is really good. I will tell you how we are lodged. Up a staircase, exactly like a ladder, we have a good-sized room, with casement windows at each end, and sanded floor. Within this room are two little rooms, 1 and 2, about four feet square. In 2 is a bed, and Madame Legoux has that to herself. In 1, we can just squeeze in our two little beds, and there we sleep. In the large room Aubin sleeps on a couch. B. dresses, and we eat, drink, and sit, but then it is all clean. We get very good soup, excellent freshwater fish, and a sort of vegetable which is excellent stewed. The roast meat is not good, and with it they bring you up apples, currant jelly, and all sorts of sweet things ; you get excellent Hock.

If I could think less of home, of England, and your own dear self, more than all, or anything else, I should be happy, and we always find something to amuse us and to laugh at. There is a little *tittupping* doctor on his travels, whom we fell in with at the inn at Engelholm, and as all English herd like sheep in a foreign country, and he is going the same way as us, we see him at the different inns. He is now waiting here to sail. He kills me, for I am convinced he means to write his travels, and he is so exactly the kind of dapper traveller whose tours one reads. Then as to H.,[4] no great fat bear could be so stupid or so useless—at all events, a bear would be bolder. We laugh at him, and every moment have some ridiculous story of him ; but, if one thought seriously about it, he deserves hanging, for the selfishness and total want of attention he has shown from the moment we left England ; for he literally thinks only of taking very good care of himself.

I must now go to bed, and shall write

---

[4] The footman.

more to-morrow. Heaven bless you! How I wish I could kiss you and hear you say good-night!

Lady Burghersh to her Mother

October 19

My dearest Mama,—I begin again this morning. The wind is the same and the weather very fine, but I do not go out, for somehow or other my cold, which was quite gone, has returned, and I am nursing it before I sail again. There is indeed nothing to tempt one out here, but they say the church is pretty. The passage from here to Stralsund is about the same as from Holyhead to Dublin. You may trace our route on the map you have got, like mine, from Engelholm (which is the place we slept at the second night from Gottenburgh) through Helsingborg, Lund, and Dalby to Ystad. Lund is the only thing like a town, except Helsingborg, on the whole road, and it is there the women dress so prettily.

I got a long letter from Princess Charlotte yesterday, *qui brûle le papier* with love. She says she is ill. . . . I shall not forget the prints for my aunt,[5] but I should like to know what was her route to and from Vienna, as it would be some guide for me. I don't think she ever went by Berlin, did she? If she would let me know that, I could be of more use, perhaps. . . .

Tuesday evening

The captain of the brig has this moment been to say the wind is fair, and we are going to embark, and shall be

[5] Mrs. Villiers, afterwards Lady Clarendon, her mother's twin sister, who had been abroad many years before for some time.

to-morrow, I hope, at Stralsund.   My cold
is better to-night, and I hope the sea-sick-
ness (which I am sure of in the brig) will
carry it quite off.   God bless you ever,
dearest Mama.

Your most truly affec.,

P.

Lady Burghersh to her Sister Emily

Stralsund : October 22, 1813

My dearest Emily,—Here we arrived
last night, and here I am as well as ever I
was, which you will wonder at when you
know all that has passed since I wrote to
Mama from Ystad on Tuesday ; but Providence protects us, and, thank God, all the
dangers and horrors of the sea are now at
an end.

I told Mama in my letter that I had
my cold still, and I had not stirred from

one hot room for three days. The doctor
I mentioned to her had prescribed for me,
and as he seemed to understand me and
be sensible, I caught at the idea of taking
him over in the ship with us, for conceive
what a risk it appeared to take me out of
this hot room at two o'clock in the morning,
put me into an open cart which was half
full of water, and thence to embark. I
went to bed the instant I got on board; my
cold did not increase at all, but the next
morning I had a great deal of fever, and
the doctor said I must positively not leave
my bed, whether the ship came to anchor
or not. As it was, we had the good luck
of a calm, and therefore, though our passage was slow—for we only arrived in Pust
Bay yesterday morning—no one was the
least sick, and we felt no motion. There
never was anything so attentive and obliging as the captain of the brig. He could,

however, only carry us as far as Pust Bay, which is in the Island of Rügen, and twenty-five English miles from Stralsund. We had our choice of landing there and getting up to Stralsund as we could in carts, or going into a ship which had the carriages on board. I had too good a lesson of scrambling up to Gottenburgh, so I chose the latter. This ship we moved into was a sort of *galliot*, a small thing with one mast; no cabin that you can go into, and the carriages are put down into a sort of hole, so that I could not sit in them, and had no alternative but to sit on deck, which appeared rather desperate just out of my bed, and it was very cold. However, there was no help for it, so I wrapped myself well up, and Madame L. and I sat in the boat on deck; we were in it from two o'clock till pitch-dark, and I gradually recovered the whole time, arrived here without fever, my cold nearly gone, and not even tired!

Now I have to tell you of a sight which certainly I might not see in a thousand years! Just as we were entering the harbour, within sight of the town, we saw a ship on fire; we did not know what it was or we should not have ventured past it, but the captain of our ship was dead drunk, and it was literally by chance that B. told the men to keep as far away as they could for fear, as he said, the guns should go off; but the passage was so narrow that we were obliged to pass very near it. It proved to be an English transport (a brig) laden with ammunition, and having on board 9,000 whole barrels of ball cartridges. As we passed her the whole stern was blazing; we were at the distance of two or three hundred yards from her, certainly not more, and I was looking intently at the flames, when she blew up. It is quite impossible to render the effect of so tremendous and so magnificent a sight, but the most extraordinary part was the minute after the explosion; the balls and splinters of the ship came rattling down like a thick shower of hail, they fell all round us, and numbers struck our ship in every part. It is hardly credible that not a soul on board was touched. Every man fell flat upon his face, except B., who was standing near me and threw himself over me to protect me. On looking up, the whole sky was covered with black smoke, and not a single vestige left of the ship; the effect on the sea was exactly as if it boiled. A little rowing boat had just passed us, and three men in it were wounded with the balls, one very badly. That is all the mischief: was there ever so miraculous an escape!

Now I will tell you what has astonished me beyond measure. I was not the least moved by it. I can hardly believe myself that not only I neither jumped nor trembled, but was wholly intent on the magnificence of the sight. And till B. threw himself over me, as I tell you, I never thought of looking away. Madame L. says she never shall forget in her life her surprise that the first thing she heard after the shock was me saying to her : '*Mais regardez donc comme c'est beau !*' She was very much frightened. The concussion shook our boat most violently ; you may think what it was when I tell you what damage it did in the town. In the house we are now in, which is certainly two miles from where the ship was, the windows are not only broken, but several of the frames with iron hoops round them were broken and thrown into

D

the rooms.   There are great heaps of
plaster lying in the passage, shaken down
from the ceiling, and the door of the room
B. dresses in is broken from the top to
the bottom.

As it was, I would not have missed
seeing it for anything ; but how curious
that it should happen at the instant of our
passing, and how curious that, after all I
have gone through, I am here this morning in the most perfect health !   Madame
L. is also quite well.

We proceed to-morrow to Berlin.' B.
found a letter here for him from C.
Stewart,[6] begging us to make use of his
house at Berlin (the English Minister's
residence), which, as he is not likely himself to want it now, we shall accept, at least
until—if we find Berlin the best place for

[6] Sir Charles Stewart (afterwards Lord Londonderry),
then Minister to Prussia, and at that moment with the
armies.

me to stay at—I can get a house of my own. It is a great relief to me, for I have seen enough of foreign inns to tremble at the idea of remaining in one for any time, and without B. really I don't think I could; and I suppose I shall have the misery of being left in Berlin while he goes up to headquarters.

This appears a fine large town; I have not been out to-day yet, but am going presently to walk about. The weather is beautiful to-day. We are in a large inn kept by an Italian; well off, so far, that the people speak French, and we have four good rooms (though there is no possibility of a fire except in one). There never was such a treasure as the little cooking machine; I regularly make use of it, for I cannot accustom myself to the garlic and onions of foreign dishes; but I get a fowl (which you find everywhere)

and boil it in the machine, and boil my
potatoes also, and have that way a good
wholesome dinner every day.

The news we hear here you will have
in England as soon as this letter, and more
circumstantially than I can give it you. It
is very great, and Bavaria having joined
the allies is excellent. They tell us of a
battle[7] fought on Tuesday, which they say
nearly annihilated Buonaparte, but I have
not yet heard if that is official or not.
God grant that it may be true, and that
B. may have little occasion to leave me!
I must leave off now, and shall add more
by and by. . . . Heaven bless you, and
kiss my dearest Mama a thousand times
for me! I don't believe anyone can imagine the misery of being so many many
days without hearing of you all. . . .

I tear open my letter to say young

[7] Leipzig.

James,[8] C. Stewart's cousin, has just come
into the room, covered with orders, beard
and sweat (!) on his way from headquarters to England, with the account of
the finest battle. He will take this!

Lady Burghersh to her Mother

Berlin : October 27

My dearest, dear Mama,— I have just
received large packets from England,
and yours and Emily's letters, . . . and
you may imagine how happy all this has
made me feel. Indeed, I wanted something to rejoice me now, as I cannot
but be very miserable at the idea of so
soon parting with B., for we have now
settled that I shall remain here while he
goes to headquarters, where I do believe
no woman could go, so I must make the

---

[8] Father of the late Lord Northbourne.

best of it, and hope he will not be absent very long at a time. I have one great comfort, that it is totally impossible that there can be another great battle, nor can Buonaparte stand on this side the Rhine, and I believe the game will very soon be up, and we may amuse ourselves as we please throughout the winter. B. remains here till he hears from headquarters, which must be three or four days, and by that time I shall ' get into my shoes' here.

Now to tell you of our journey. I don't think language can express the state of the roads from Stralsund to Strelitz. They are reckoned the worst in Germany, and heavy rains for several days had rendered them almost impassable. What with dawdles, and delays of the German post-boys, we did not get away from Stralsund till four o'clock on Saturday, and we got

one stage that night to Greifswalde ; we
were eight hours doing four German miles
(about twenty English). Next day we were
nineteen hours in the carriage, and the
roads of the kind that to sleep is quite
impossible. We only stopped for three
hours each night, and for dinner in the
middle of the day, and yet I was not at
all tired, though we travelled from six in
the morning till two or three the next
morning ; but we had the carriage open
a good deal.

The second night we slept at Brandenburg, going by Anclam and Friedland. I
must tell you that at Friedland, where we
arrived about nine or ten at night, I went
into the post-house while the horses were
putting to. There were three or four
men in it looking at a print of Lord
Wellington, and talking of him with great
admiration. When we came in, they

greeted us as English, and told us who they were talking of, when one of them said he did not believe the print was like Lord Wellington, as he had heard he was an elderly man, and blind of one eye!

Monday we stopped for two hours at Strelitz. B. went to wait on the Duke of Cumberland, and carry him some letters, and he came to the inn to see me, and sat a long time with me. . . . Strelitz is a pretty and very clean town, and the country about it very pretty, with an immense quantity of fine wood, and a most beautiful lake about a mile long near the town. I walked round the palace, which is very large, but like an old barrack, and wretched ill-kept gardens to it.

We slept Monday night at Zehdemik, and arrived here yesterday at seven o'clock. We stopped at Oranienburg to dine, and went to see the palace there,

which is the *wreck* of a very fine one ; but
it has been completely sacked and ruined
by the French, and is quite a melancholy
object. The Crown Prince's[9] headquarters
were there last month. We were very
unlucky not to be here two days sooner,
when the King of Prussia[1] made his public
entry here : they say there never was anything so fine as the enthusiasm with which
he was received. He is perfectly adored
here. There was a *Te Deum*, and in the
evening he went to the opera, where everyone belonging to the Court *hired* their
boxes to give the profits to the wounded.
This morning he returns to the army.

It is certainly a most interesting mo
ment to be here. Everything is so enthusiastic, and there is a patriotism and
eagerness of which we have no idea in

---

[9] Bernadotte, then Crown Prince of Sweden.
[1] Frederick William III.

England, nor have we a conception what
these poor people have sacrificed in the
good cause ; for the poverty and wretchedness to which they have reduced themselves are quite shocking. There are now
38,000 wounded in this town, and the
princesses and ladies have many of them
sold their jewels to assist them. I hear
that at Princess Radziwill's,[2] where there is
an assembly every night, they all scrape
lint to send to the hospitals, where there
is so much wanted that it is really necessary they should do it. *Tout respire le
militaire* throughout the country. We
met numbers of prisoners on the road.
The King of Saxony with his wife and
daughter were brought in here prisoners,
the day before yesterday. The King of
Prussia lodged him in his palace, but he

[2] Princess Louisa, daughter of Prince Ferdinand of
Prussia.

still persists in declaring his allegiance to
Buonaparte. This day, 4,000 prisoners,
with Laureston, Regnier,[3] &c. who were
taken at Leipzig, march in here where
there are already princes and dukes without end, for there never was such a *crash*
as the Leipzig business.

We are most comfortably lodged in a
very fine house in the Linden, which is the
public walk of Berlin. I have seen nothing as yet of the town, for I was determined to begin writing to you directly. . .
The house is beautiful and immensely
large. It appears to me like an enchanted
castle after the horrid huts we have been
in for so long. Tom Tyrwhitt is here,
and spent a long time with us last night,
putting us *au fait* of everything, and very
entertaining he was. He remains here,
which I am glad of, as I shall feel more

[3] French marshals.

comfortable with someone here that I know. . . .

To-night I think I shall go to the theatre, and perhaps, if I can summon courage, to Princess Radziwill's afterwards, but I have such a dread of seeing and being seen for the first time, yet I must make acquaintances before B. goes, the idea of which, I own, makes me tremble, but I know from all the accounts of head-quarters that my attempting to go with him would be madness. . . .

I own I never have flagged in courage or spirits till now, and I do find them fail me at the idea of remaining here alone; but I don't give way, and I am more convinced every day how right I was in coming here, for if increased affection and gratitude from any human being can satisfy one, I ought to be so with B., and if we both feel so much at a separation which at most will not exceed a few weeks, what would it have been if I had stayed in England ; so all is for the best.

Pray say everything most affectionate from me to Mrs. V.,[4] and tell her I believe we owe our legs to her idea of having everything in the carriage strapped down, for I really think they would otherwise have been broken. Lord A.'s cushion is the very comfort of my life, and when you see him, pray tell him so. I must now end, as B. and T. Tyrwhitt are waiting for me to walk about the town. Heaven bless you, my dearest and best Mama!

Lady Burghersh to her Sister Emily

Berlin : October 28

My dearest Emily,—I have to thank you for your letter and to tell you of our

[4] Mrs. Villiers.

proceedings since I wrote to Mama yesterday.

I went out and walked all over the town, which is the most beautiful I ever saw. The buildings are quite magnificent, and not one or two of them, but at every step the most beautiful palaces and buildings of all kinds. The gate which leads to Charlottenburg [5] is the finest thing I ever saw. The Linden, where we live, is a long double alley of trees, with this gate at the end and very fine houses on each side. The King's palace, the arsenal, the churches, &c., are superb. You see but few equipages, but quantities of soldiers of all kinds and Cossacks in plenty, both officers and men, and all the greatest beasts I ever saw! The ladies walk a great deal in the Linden with bonnets that you must *see* to con-

[5] The Brandenburg gate.

ceive, for they are really a mile high and ten miles round, and many of them with ten and twelve feathers on the top! They either wear these bonnets or go without anything at all on their heads, which is quite astonishing, for the intense cold here is beyond anything I ever felt. I have been obliged to take to worsted stockings.

I went yesterday to the theatre. It is about the size of Covent Garden, perhaps rather bigger. It is reckoned the best-lighted theatre in Germany, but it appeared to me wretchedly dark, having only one large lustre hanging in the centre and one small one in the Royal box, which was in the middle of the house. The old Princess of Orange and her daughter the Princess of Brunswick were in the Royal box, but in a side box the King (who has delayed his return to the army for a day or two) was with his sister, the young Princess of Orange. It was so dark that I could not see him well, though we were just opposite.

The house is dirty; but the fine theatre, the Opera, is not now open, which I am very sorry for.

They gave three pieces last night— the first was a German play which bored me, of course, as I could not understand a word; the second was a little musical farce, and, though there were no fine singers, the orchestra is so perfect and the music so good, that I was very much pleased. The last piece, a ballet, or rather pantomime, the dancers very mediocre; but there were two grotesque dancers, sort of buffoons, who amused me very much, and the music was very good. It is all over at nine, and begins at six.

I own I don't like the hours here, for

one's whole morning is cut up, and one does not know what to do between dinner and evening, for every one dines at three o'clock. This morning we received an invitation to dine with the Dowager Princess of Orange at three, but soon after the King sent to desire B. would dine with him at Charlottenburg at two, so I was left to make my appearance at the Princess of O.'s by myself. Before I went to dress I received about a thousand visits, amongst others old Mr. and Madame Néale, and Pauline,[6] who was enchanted to see me, and who enchanted me by talking of all of you.

. . . At three o'clock I arrived at the Princess of Orange's and was shyer than

---

[6] Countess Pauline Néale, who survived until 1870, had in early life been attached to the Court of Queen Louise. She was a remarkable figure in Berlin society for over half a century. Her father was of Irish extraction, and she had many English connections.

E

shy.   There was only herself and the
Princess of Brunswick, with three ladies
and three gentlemen belonging to them,
T. Tyrwhitt, myself, and Aubin.   They
were all particularly kind to me—the old
Princess is very pleasing and good-
humoured, and talked to me a great deal
of Lady Anne,[7] Lady Mornington,[8] &c.,
&c., whom she knew in England.   She
said the Queen [9] had desired her (in the
letter she sent her by us) to show me
every kindness, as I was a person *qui
l'intéressait beaucoup.*   The Princess of
Brunswick asked me numerous questions
about *feu sa belle-mère,*[1] *sa belle-sœur,*[2] &c.,
&c., and told me she knew my mother

[7] Lady Anne Culling Smith, only sister of the Duke
of Wellington, and aunt to Lady Burghersh.

[8] Her grandmother.

[9] Queen Charlotte.

[1] The Dowager-Duchess of Brunswick, George III.'s
sister.

[2] Princess of Wales (Queen Caroline).

had shown the greatest kindness to
Madame Haeckel. They are just like
the Windsor Royalties, for they literally
know everything, and seemed completely
au fait of my family, for the Princess of
O. said she knew I had lived a great
deal at Blackheath, knew exactly how
long I had been married, &c., &c. They
are all very inquisitive about Princess
Charlotte, and seem to be completely
aware of all her good qualities. . . .

The dinner was over in a trice, and
(as I am not yet used to putting half a
dozen plates round me) I was nearly
starved. B. arrived about five from Charlottenburg, and soon after we were *con-
gédié.* It is the custom here to pay visits
after dinner, so we drove to Madame
Zichy's, a very good-humoured, gay,
pleasing woman, not pretty, who talks
English without the least accent, and

seemed a sort of person to like. We are now come home to amuse ourselves as we can till eight, which is the hour to go to Princess Louisa's, and it is lucky for me to have this moment to write, as I find the courier sets off to-night. To-morrow we are asked to dine with Princess Ferdinand of Prussia, the King's aunt.

As B. has not heard yet from Lord Aberdeen or C. Stewart, I do not know exactly when he will go. Of all those I have seen, I like best Pauline Néale's mother, who talked to me with so much feeling, and seemed really anxious to be motherly that she quite won my heart. I should enjoy seeing everything so new if it was not for the idea of so soon being left, and I am obliged to summon up all my courage to go through it all as I do. To-day I saw an immense number of prisoners go by. I never saw such wretched sights : many of them quite boys, and so haggard, so sickly, and almost bare!

Wellington is in every mouth here, and the perfect idol. . . . I am looking most eagerly for the opening of Hamburg, for if it is not open before the frost sets in, the communication by Sweden will be stopped, and we may be many weeks without news from England. God forbid it should be so!

Lady Burghersh to her Mother

Berlin : October 30, 1813

My dearest Mama,—For the first time since my letter to E. was finished Thursday last, I find a moment to begin this letter, which will be sent—God knows when, but I am obliged to keep ready as the couriers from headquarters often stop only an hour here. We are just returned from dining at Count Zichy's, and, thank God! spend the evening at home.

B. has not heard a word yet from Lord Aberdeen or C. Stewart, although an estafette was sent to the latter the moment we arrived. We cannot account for such a delay, but I am very glad of it, as it keeps B. here a little longer. The idea is that the armies are still pursuing the French, which would prevent their writing.

Since I wrote last, I have made acquaintance with most persons at Berlin, and I must say one and all show me the greatest kindness and attention. Thursday evening I went for the first time to Princess Louisa's,[3] who receives every night. She is quite adored here, and is *the* person who makes society here. She is

[3] Radziwill.

ugly (even like Lady ——, only not *so*
ugly), but particularly pleasing, and with
no sort of form about her. Her husband,
Prince Radziwill, is much the most agreeable man I have seen here, and they have
a great many beautiful children, particularly
a little girl of ten years old, who is the
most graceful little creature I ever saw,[4]
and who has taken a great fancy to me.
The youngest, a baby of nine months old,
is beautiful. I cannot say the 'Société'
is very gay, and I never saw such an
assemblage of ugly women. I assure
you P—— N—— is quite good-looking
amongst them! . . .

The Princess has a large basket near
her filled with linen, and everybody
takes a bit and picks it to pieces for lint,
and it is surprising the immense quantity

[4] Elisa Radziwill, the early love of the Emperor
William. She died young.

there appears at the end of the evening. Certainly the inhabitants of this town have shown a *dévouement* to the good cause which is admirable. The ladies of the highest rank attend at the hospitals. Princess Louisa told me yesterday that she had several wounded officers in her own palace, and that yesterday morning she had attended two of them when they were dressed. The women hardly dress at all smartly, as all *luxe* was laid aside during the horrors of the war when it was carried on under the walls of Berlin, and has not been taken up since. They were saying yesterday that no ladies were now seen to ride in Berlin, as all superfluous horses have been sent by them to the armies. It is impossible not to catch an enthusiasm so general. I was happy when the first evening was over. Yesterday we dined at Princess Ferdinand's, who

is Princess Louisa's mother. You must
have heard of her, for she was mother,
too, of Prince Louis.[5] I never saw such
a formal, stiff, disagreeable old woman—
vieille cour outrée, and she frightened me
to death. I was glad to get away, and
go again to Princess Louisa's, who had
dined there with us. I liked that evening
much better than the first, for there were
only six or seven persons. . . .

The Princess showed me some pic-
tures of the late Queen of Prussia, who
must have been beautiful. The King,
who adored her, and who seems to be the
most amiable private character possible,
is still miserable at her loss, and never
misses a day visiting her tomb at Charlottenburg.

To-day we had a dinner quite *à l'anglaise* at Count Zichy's, with roast beef and

---

[5] Killed at Jena.

a wood fire! . . . This morning I went
to the Porcelain Manufactory, and stayed
three hours looking at the most beautiful
things I ever beheld. I think I shall
spend half my life there. There is a dinner service making for Charles Stewart,
which the master of the manufactory said
surpasses everything they have yet made.
Every plate and dish is different, and the
painting the finest that can be conceived,
but it is enormously expensive. They say
this service will cost between one and two
thousand pounds! They have heads of
Lord Wellington on many pieces of china,
but none like, so I have promised to give
them a print and medal to copy from, under
my directions. I bought nothing there
to-day but some blue china necklaces,
which I thought pretty, and which I mean
to send over to you by the first opportunity, but I am sorry to say it is very

difficult to convey anything to England, and particularly china. . . .

I don't yet know, except the china, what Berlin produces, as I have not been into a single shop. I reserve it all to amuse me when B. is gone.

This house is in the most delightful situation for gazing, for everything comes by it. I saw Lauriston, Régnier, and Bertrand[6] brought in. Bertrand lodges at an hotel a few doors off. He was very much insulted by the populace, as he was the man who was promised the title of Duke of Berlin if he should take Berlin. They cried out to him, 'Here comes the Duke of Berlin, take him to the hangman!' He has never dared to go out since; the others go about and go to the theatre. This morning I saw 5,000 prisoners come in with a great many officers and a quantity

6 French marshals who had been made prisoners.

of wounded; the latter were a sickening sight.

Not having heard anything, my plans are of course as unfixed as before, but meantime I am most comfortably lodged here. My apartments consist of two large ante-rooms, then the room I sit in, which opens on one side into a magnificent large room with gilt panels, where we dine and breakfast; on the other side into the bed-room, with a fine blue satin bed; beyond that a dressing-room, another large ante-room, and then Madame Legoux's room. All these look into the Linden. On the other side of the house, which is built round a square, there is another suite of rooms all on the same floor. . . .

The cold is extreme, but so dry and bracing that it is a pleasure to be out. I cannot bear the stoves: one always feels stived, and then it is so dull not to see the fire. . . . Words can't describe the figures the women dress here of a morning. Figure to yourself the most fashionable hat, black, with at least six and often ten or twelve very high feathers, an immense quilling of lace or ribbon round the poke, and enormous bows wherever they can be stuck. A pelisse of some very glaring colour of satin wadded, and the sleeves tied like those in England, but immensely full.[7] As every woman wears these hats, my little cottage bonnet is so stared at that I really believe I must get one to walk about in. P. in one is much higher from her chin upwards than downwards !

November 1

B. has at last had a letter from C. Stewart. The armies have advanced with

[7] A rough sketch accompanying this letter shows the fashions here described to have closely resembled those of the present day !

most wonderful rapidity, and will, I think, have reached Frankfurt before B. gets there. He sets off to-morrow; I need not say what I feel about it, because you must know it requires no common courage to think even of my forlorn situation here, which is rendered for the moment ten times worse by the advance of the armies towards the Rhine, as, though it is such good news for the cause, it removes him so much further from me. However, it is no use brooding over such melancholy subjects which cannot be remedied.

.   .   .   .   .

A break here occurs in the letters— three or four having evidently been lost or destroyed. After Lord Burghersh had left her she remained nearly three weeks without any news of him or knowing where he was. At last, news came of his having joined the Austrian headquarters on their way to Frankfurt, and by this

time she had become so tired of her life of
idle suspense and uncertainty at Berlin,
that she determined to set off to join him
at Frankfurt. Fortunately for her, Sir T.
Tyrwhitt (the English officer mentioned in
her letters from Berlin) was going to headquarters, and offered to escort her, for she
could not have ventured on a journey along
the line of the French retreat without
protection of some sort. The journey is
described in two letters to her mother,
the first being dated from

Weimar : November 21, 1813

My dearest Mama,—Being detained
here for want of horses, I cannot do better
than begin a letter to you which I shall
finish at Frankfurt.

Last Tuesday I took leave of all my
friends in Berlin, and dined at Princess
Louisa's. I am in violent favour, and
received the most tender *embrassades*,

assurances of eternal friendship, and all kinds of compliments, &c., &c.

Next morning, before I set off, I received a ring from Princess Louisa, with joined hands, but, notwithstanding all their kindness, I left Berlin with real joy. We set off on Wednesday morning in the midst of a heavy snow, which, however, did not last.

I will give you our route to this place, as you may like to trace it on the map. The first day through Potsdam to Brandenburg ; the second day through Ziethen to Zerbst ; the third day we crossed the Elbe at Dessau, and slept at Halle ; and yesterday we went through Merseburg, Weissenfels, and Naumburg, and slept at Auerstadt. We shall get to Frankfurt Wednesday, and never did any poor creature long more eagerly to get to any place than I do to arrive there, for I have gone through a great deal, and it required no little courage to undertake such a journey. Think what comfort for me to hear on the morning of my leaving Berlin that the armies had left Frankfurt and crossed the Rhine in pursuit of the French, and, till I arrived here to-day, I had no idea where B. was likely to be or what was doing, for there is no information to be got on the road. I expected to find a letter from him here, but there is not one. I am, however, amply repaid for that disappointment by finding that the two Emperors and King remain at Frankfurt ; therefore I shall find him there, and my joy at this may be conceived !

You will see we have not gone through Leipzig. It is in such a state from the numbers of unburied bodies remaining from the battle, that we were advised not to approach it, and, God knows, we have

F

seen horrors enough without seeking more.
We have come all along the line of the
French retreat, and as it is not a month
since they passed, the roads are covered
with dead horses and remains of dead men.
The latter, I am told, we shall see many
of between this and Frankfurt, particularly
at Hanau, where Wrede fought his san-
guinary battle a fortnight ago. No language can describe the horrible devasta-
tion these French have left behind them,
and without seeing it no one can form an
idea of the country through which such a
retreat as theirs has been made. Every
bridge blown up, every village burnt or
pulled down, fields completely devastated,
orchards all turned up, and we traced their
bivouaques all along by every horror you
can conceive. None of the country people
will bury them or their horses, so there
they remain lying all over the fields and

roads, with millions of crows feasting—we passed quantities, bones of all kinds, hats, shoes, epaulettes, a surprising quantity of rags and linen—every kind of horror.

At Dessau, and below, we crossed on bridges of boats (rather nervous work), and at Weissenfels we went over a bridge of rafts only, which was thrown over a very wide river, the Saale, in three hours' time, for General Blücher to pursue the French, who had hardly time to get out of the town, and Buonaparte hid himself in a mill. They told us that the French soldiers were in such a state of starvation that they took the earrings from their ears and implored for bits of bread, which none of the inhabitants would give them. The consequence is the river is full of bodies; we found Halle full of wounded; there being 14,000 in that town.

There was but one room to be had

in the inn, which was also quite full
of wounded Russians, and smelling! oh,
heavens! I got that room for myself and
Madame Legoux, and T. Tyrwhitt per-
suaded some Prussian officers to give up
another to him and his secretary.

I took precautions before I left Berlin,
and got some sulphureous powder which
is burnt in the hospitals to purify the air.
I also wear quantities of camphor and my
dear little aromatic vinegar-box, and make
Madame L. do the same. Never was
such a treasure to me as she is, or any
creature so attentive, so amiable, and such
a comfort as I find her in the midst of all
my troubles. We have not seen a single
traveller on the road. We meet nothing
but Cossacks and troops going to join
the grand army, and a few deserters and
stragglers from the French. The country
from Merseburg here is very fine where

the French have not devastated it. We passed over the field of the battle of Jena.

At Auerstadt, where we slept last night, the French passed a night on their retreat, and have left it but the remains of a ruined village. They burnt half the houses, pulled many entirely to pieces, and left them heaps of ruins. They sacked everything, and did not leave a cow or chicken even in the town. The place where we slept was saved, as the poor woman told us, by the kindness of a Polish general, who preserved her house from being burnt or pulled down, but could not save all her hay, which she said was worth 600 dollars, all her poultry, her cows, six horses, and everything the house contained, for we found in it scarcely anything but straw strewed as in a stable. The room I slept in was occupied by

Oudinot, and T. Tyrwhitt's by Victor.[8] Buonaparte slept at an apothecary's shop over the way.

Instead of complaining at all they have suffered, and which years cannot repair, these fine people seem really to have but one sentiment—devotion to the cause, and abhorrence of the French name. They laugh at their King Jerome,[9] and say they do not think he will visit them again soon.

I must wish you good-night, my dearest, dear Mama, for I am very sleepy, and must be up long before daylight to-morrow. I am perfectly well, not the least tired, and look forward with such delight to the end of all these melancholy sights at Frankfurt; for, as I don't think I am likely to follow them into France, I shall

[8] French marshals.

[9] Napoleon's brother, Jerome Buonaparte, King of Westphalia.

there end my travels over a line of retreat, and shall then again be with B. Sir T. Tyrwhitt is as obliging and kind as possible. Heaven bless you! I shall continue this at Frankfurt.

Lady Burghersh to her Mother

Frankfurt : Friday, November 26

Here we arrived to-day, my dearest Mama, but I consider my journey as over since yesterday, as it was yesterday I had the happiness of finding B. at Hanau, where we slept. But I will go on regularly and tell you of our expedition from Weimar.

We got horses on Monday morning, but we could not get *schwagers*,[1] so we had peasants to drive us. These peasants knew nothing of the road, which is rather intricate, as it is necessary to avoid the

[1] Postboys.

vicinity of Erfurt, where the French garrison is 6,000 strong. We were going on
when we saw an officer galloping very
hard towards us, and making us signs to
stop. He was a Prussian officer, who
came up to us very civilly, and asked us if
we were aware that we were going right
into Erfurt,[2] which was not above half
an English mile off. Conceive what an
escape ! We were already at the outposts
of the Prussians, and they came to guide
us through their bivouaques round the
town. We were close to the trenches,
which are opened in front of the town ;
the bombarding was expected to begin the
next day. As we were so near we got out
of the carriage and walked all through the
army and along the trenches, and on the
parapet we could see close into the town.

[2] Which was occupied by the French and besieged
by the allies.

The officers, with their suite, &c., came out to us, and were very civil. It was very amusing, and so new to me ; but the worst part of the day was to come. We were obliged to go over the country, and that is in such a state that it was necessary to get out of the carriage and have it held up by two or three men to prevent it overturning. After being out the whole day we got at night to a village (one of the outposts), where we hoped to get horses and go on to Gotha. We found this village destroyed by a *sortie* of the French. No horses to be got, nor even any fodder for the poor creatures that drew us. We were therefore obliged to drag on to another most wretched village, the headquarters of General Ziethen, with 2,000 soldiers in it, and about three English miles from Erfurt. Here we had no alternative, for stop we must. A very civil old man and woman came out, and offered us one room in their miserable cottage. In that and the yard were already quartered twenty-eight soldiers. The one room was at the top of the house, without fire, and the window broken. Here we made up our minds to pass the night—that is, T. Tyrwhitt, his secretary, and me; for my carriage, in which was Madame Legoux, with everything belonging to me, had got more sensible peasants to drive, and they got safely to Gotha in good time. In this room, then, in one of the coldest November nights, I lay down on the carriage cushions spread on the floor, and covered with a great coat. T. Tyrwhitt spent the night in the kitchen.

I slept well, caught no cold, and set off merrily next morning. At Gotha we found poor Madame Legoux, who had been in a fine fuss about us. I also found a courier from B., telling me he would meet me at Hanau, one stage from this place. Think how bad the communication is with Berlin that he never got my *estafette*, and only knew of my coming through Charles Stewart, who arrived here from Hanover some days ago.

The horrors of the road increased at every step as we approached Hanau. We made the postboys holloa out when we were coming to any dead bodies, so I escaped seeing many. I only saw five, which came upon me unawares ; four of them were stripped of all clothing, two nearly skeletons. As to the horses, they lay ten and twelve together, and in some places the stench was horrid. But at Hanau it all ended in my joy at finding B. again! This morning we came here. The town is as full as it can hold—emperors, kings, princes, without end. We are in a very bad quarter, and with great difficulty got any at all; but to-morrow we are to change into a very good one, which C. Stewart has insisted on giving up to us.

The Grand Duchess of Weimar is, I believe, the only woman here, but I can tell you little of the persons here, having been only a few hours in the town, and I am so very happy to find myself with B. that I am as yet quite bewildered.

Is it not extraordinary that after such a journey of nine days, getting up every morning two hours before daylight, and travelling till eight, nine, or ten at night, I am not only not the least tired, but grown fat! Both Pozzo[3] and C. Stewart were quite struck with my looking so much better than in London. C. Stewart

[3] Count Pozzo di Borgo, a Corsican diplomatist in the Russian service. He had been much in England, and was a friend of all Lady Burghersh's family.

looks shockingly ; Pozzo much as usual, with a fine Russian general's uniform.

C. Stewart has behaved beautifully in every way, and shown the most real friendship for both B. and me. He has had an opportunity of showing it to B., who has been most abominably used by ——, who has done everything in his power to undermine him with the great folks and to put another person in his shoes. It is a long story, and can't be entered into in a letter, but I must say B. has behaved like an *angel*, and I must think if there is any justice he will gain great credit at home as he has done here for his moderation and good sense. He is so happy to have me again, and I really hope there is every chance of their all staying here quietly some time longer. If they should move, I believe I should go to Stuttgardt.

I have had a great disappointment in

not finding letters here from you. It is such an age since I have had such a happiness, but B. has sent many letters which arrived here to Berlin, so I must wait till they are returned from thence. My dearest, dear Mama, do you know how hard it is to wait for them, for I never have you out of my thoughts, and a letter is such a happiness! Oh, if I could give you one kiss, dearest Mama! I send this off by young Woronzow, who sets off to-night for England—happy man! God bless you and all of you a thousand times!

Lady Burghersh to ——

Frankfurt : December 3

. . . I must now tell you how we are going on here. . . . We are as well lodged as possible in the best part of the town, and have a very pretty suite of rooms—three very nice drawing-rooms. I lead a curious life, and yet an interesting and agreeable one, but I never see a woman, except a visit of ceremony to the two Grand Duchesses and the Princess of Tour and Taxis; they are the only ladies here. The two first are sisters of the Emperor of Russia,[4] and both in their different ways delightful. The Grand Duchess Catherine, who is widow of the young Prince of Oldenburg, has the most delightful expression of mildness I ever saw. The other, the Grand Duchess Maria, is married to the Prince of Weimar, and is pretty. The Princess Tour and Taxis is our Queen's niece,[5] and sister to the late Queen of Prussia.[6] I see her often.

[4] Alexander.   [5] Queen Charlotte.

[6] Queen Louise, who died in 1810, celebrated for her beauty and misfortunes—mother of the old Emperor William.

All the Ambassadors have given
dinners for me.   The first was at C.
Stewart's, where I was presented to
twenty-five men, all the big-wigs here
who manage the destinies of the world!
Schwarzenberg,[7] the Commander-in-Chief
of the Allies, Metternich,[8] Hardenberg,[9]
&c., &c.   Lord Cathcart gave one the
next day, and Lord Aberdeen the day
after.   Conceive how odd for me to be
the only woman at table with from fifteen
to thirty men!   I found it dreadful at
first, but now I am quite used to it, and
of course I am such a *rara avis* that I
have all the fuss possible made with me.

To-day I saw a very fine sight.   It
was the day of the *fête* of the Emperor
of Russia's own regiment.   There was a

[7] Prince Charles Schwarzenberg, Austrian field-
marshal.

[8] The famous Austrian diplomatist.

[9] Prussian Minister of State.

grand parade, and after that a mass performed. I was at both. It is impossible
to conceive a more magnificent sight than
the Emperor's Body Guard—all the finest,
tallest men that can be picked out, and his
own guard of Cossacks quite beautiful.

The Emperor of Russia,[1] the Emperor
of Austria,[2] and the King of Prussia, all
came to the parade together on horseback,
followed by a concourse of generals and
officers, all in full uniform, with their
orders, &c., and making as fine a sight
as possible. After the regiments had
passed they all dismounted, and we went
to hear the mass in a room. It is very
extraordinary and very beautiful. The
singing of the Russian soldiers is inde-
scribably beautiful, all bass voices, but so
well in tune, and so kept under, that the
effect is like soft instruments. When the

---

[1] Alexander I.   [2] Francis I.

G

Emperor passes them, instead of huzza-
ing, they shout in a very particular
manner, but very fine, I think, and then
their bands are perfect.

I must now give you some account
of some of the great people. The Royalties I did not see till to-day, as the
Emperor Alexander only returned yesterday from a visit to Carlsruhe, and the
King has also been absent. I was as
much examined as *I* examined, and I am
told I gave satisfaction, and that I am
threatened with a great dinner at Schwarzenberg's to create better acquaintance.
I never was so disappointed as in the
Emperor Alexander. He is the image of
———, only fair instead of red, and also
very like W., the dentist. He has certainly fine shoulders, but beyond that he
is horridly ill-made. He holds himself
bent quite forward, for which reason all

his Court imitate him and bend too, and
gird in their waists like women! His
countenance is not bad, and that is all
I can say of him. The Emperor of Austria is a little wizened old man, not to be
known from the D—— of G——; but as
for the King of Prussia, I never saw a
more interesting-looking person. Without being handsome, there is a fine
soldierlike look about his whole figure,
and a quiet, melancholy expression of
countenance which interests one directly.
I don't know anyone like him. He has
two sons with him—very nice boys.[3]
Then I must not forget the Grand Duke
Constantine. He is like the Emperor of
Russia, but without exception the greatest
monster I ever saw in a human form.
Then come the Grand Duke of Weimar,

[3] Afterwards King Frederick William IV. and the
Emperor William I. They were then respectively eighteen and sixteen years old.

Prince Paul of Würtemberg, the Elector
of Hesse, &c., &c.   Old Platow,[4] the
finest old weatherbeaten face I ever saw,
and very like the little prints I had of
him in London.   Barclay de Tolly,[5] an
ugly old fellow ; Miloradowitch, Czernicheff,[6] and old Blücher, who never was
beat, and to whom the allies certainly owe
much of their success ; Uvaroff, Alexander's favourite, and the same who murdered Paul.[7]   He looks like a savage, and
I could hardly bear to speak to him at
dinner.   Besides these great sights, I see
a great deal—Prince Radziwill, who is
come from Berlin to see the fun, young
Esterhazy,[8] &c., &c.   I ride every day,

---

[4] 'Hetman' of the Cossacks, a great Russian commander.

[5] Another Russian general.

[6] Russian and Polish commanders.

[7] The Russian Emperor Paul 1. was murdered by his
own officers in 1803.

[8] The same who was afterwards Austrian ambassador
in England, and famous for his jewels.

though our own horses are not yet come,
but C. Stewart has lent me one of his—
much the most perfect horse I ever rode,
perfectly safe and quiet, and I have re-
gained all my courage. . . . It is a great
beauty, and an interesting horse too, for it
has been in the great battles.

.   .   .   .   .   .

The plan of campaign seems now to
be decided for Switzerland, but I have
every reason to hope the headquarters
won't move for some time, as it must take
a long time to prepare for such a movement, and I am as well and as happy here
as I can be under the circumstances.

.   .   .   .   .   .

The surrender of Pampeluna is delightful, but we hear from France of a
battle [9] in which Lord Wellington has been
most victorious. Platow has offered to

[9] Passage of the Nivelle, November 10, 1813.

go with 1,500 Cossacks across France,
and to meet Lord Wellington. If allowed,
he would accomplish it, for those Cossacks
can do anything, and they are so feared
that a whole regiment flies before a hand-
ful. They are terrible thieves ; they steal
everything they see, and you always see
them leading, in the most barefaced
manner, two or three horses laden with
plunder.

There is a very good theatre here,
where I go very often. The orchestra is
perfect, and some of the singers very
good.   I heard the ' Flauto Magico ' done
beautifully last night. This morning there
was a distribution of medals to every
Russian who served in the campaign of
1812, from the Emperor down to the
lowest soldier.   They are very pretty—
silver medals hung to light blue ribbon.
It is not unusual to see men in the ranks

with three or four orders, and surely it is
a means of encouraging them.

Lady Burghersh to her Mother

Frankfurt : December 6, 1813

My dearest Mama,—As I sent off
only yesterday letters both to you and
my sisters, I can have but little to say
to-day, but I must send a line by Pozzo,
who is to set off in the course of to-night.
He will have the happiness of seeing you
(how I envy him!), and you will hear from
him how well and strong I am. I fear,
however, that my quiet, agreeable existence here will soon end. After such discussions and disputes as must exist in
such a headquarters as this, where there
are so many great people, and not one
great head to whom the others look up,
I believe they have decided to move from

hence towards Switzerland directly. Next
Friday is the day named for Schwarzenberg's departure, and we of course move
with him. Freiburg will be the headquarters. I cannot yet say whether I
shall go there directly, or stop for a time
at Stuttgardt. That must depend upon
the plan of operations, which is as yet
dans l'air. The indecision and squab-
bling about it among all the different
chiefs is incredible, and as long as they
can't agree nothing can be done. I am
certainly very sorry to move from here,
though, as a soldier, I am sure we have
been here much too long, and let *the*
moment escape. If Lord Wellington had
been here, he would not have hesitated.

We have just heard of the Prince of
Orange's reception in Holland. When I
hear of the expedition to be sent from
England, I can't help rejoicing that we

are here,, but there are moments when the sort of longing I have for home cannot be described—in short, I can only live *au jour la journée,* for I dare not look forward from one week to another. B. is quite well, and must, I think, have gained great credit by his conduct here.

I must leave off, for I am just going to the Grand Duchess Catherine's. It is her *jour de fête,*[1] and everybody goes this evening to *faire leurs compliments.* I have this instant received your letters! How dear your expressions are about my safety! I must end. &c., &c.

Lady Burghersh to her Mother

Frankfurt : December 10, 1813

My dearest Mama, — Our departure is now decided. Prince Schwarzenberg

---

[1] November 25, St. Catherine's day by Russian Calendar.

set off late last night or early this morning ;
the Emperors go on Sunday, and we also
set off the day after to-morrow for Freiburg. We shall probably go by Stuttgardt.
As they think to get possession of Switzerland by negotiation, they don't expect any
active operations yet. I must say how
very civil and obliging I have found all
the great people about my following the
headquarters. The moment the going
was decided on, late on Tuesday night,
Schwarzenberg sent to me to tell me, and
to say he hoped I meant to go with them,
and he would take care I had good
quarters, and everything I could want.
Independent of being with B., I am so
interested in all that goes on, and in all
their negotiations, that I should be quite
miserable to leave them, and I am now
quite used to the sort of life.

I spent nearly an hour yesterday morning with 'Sa Majesté Impériale Alexandre,' and in a way which made me better acquainted with him than I should have been in meeting him thirty times *en société.* The Grand Duchess Catherine (whom I quite delight in) sent to desire I would go to her at one o'clock. I found the Emperor with her. She said she hoped I would forgive *cette petite surprise,* as the Emperor wished very much to know me, and she was sure I should not dislike such a *connaissance.* As there was only herself, him, and me, we soon got intimate ; he gave me a whole account of last year's campaign,[2] with a great deal of modesty as to himself and his people, and then made the most violent panegyrics upon Lord Wellington, saying, '*Ah ! si nous avions un capitaine comme celui-là, nous aurions bien*

---

[2] Napoleon's famous Russian campaign and burning of Moscow.

mieux fait.' I said I did not think it was
possible to *mieux faire.* '*Ah, Madame,
c'est que le bon Dieu nous a servi de capitaine et que l'exemple des Anglais nous a
donné du courage.'* I was much better
pleased with him than I expected. His
manners have much less *fanfaronnade*
than I had imagined, and his countenance
is certainly very delightful. When he is
animated and smiles, his mouth and chin
remind me immensely of Sir H. Mildmay ;
he has the same particular curl in his upper
lip—do you know what I mean ? Nevertheless, I can't think him handsome, and
his voice is rough and disagreeable.

In the evening there was a great ball
given by the Russians at the Assembly
Room, which was beautifully decorated
with orange trees and shrubs of all kinds.
The ladies (besides the Grand Duchesses)
were collected from Frankfurt and its

environs. There were, of course, few compared with the number of men, but these in all their different uniforms and orders made it brilliant and magnificent. I was so dreadfully abashed when I first went in that I thought I should have died, and don't know what I should have done but for that most charming Grand Duchess Catherine, who was very near as bad as me, as she had not been out before since her husband's death, and we supported each other.

The ball began with polonaises, which are in fact only *walking* in time. I danced (or walked) one with the Emperor Alexander, one with Prince Paul of Würtemberg, and another with General Czernicheff, of whom you may have heard. Then came a set of English country dances, which I danced with Prince Radziwill. After that waltzing; they all waltz as quick, if not quicker, than Madame Lieven. I would not try it. There were also quadrilles. . . .

The King of Prussia talked to me. He is very shy, but notwithstanding that there is an expression of goodness and amiableness very delightful. I was introduced for the first time to the Emperor Francis—rather a nice old man, and not at all unlike Lord Clarendon when he speaks. I never saw two nicer boys than the King of Prussia's two sons, particularly the elder—a merry, good-humoured creature. The King has also a nephew of the Queen's with him, who is also great-nephew to *our* Queen, and who, I am told, they want Princess Charlotte to marry. He is very young, but as handsome and as pleasing a lad as I ever saw.

I have made lately another acquaintance which I delight in — old General

Blücher. He is the picture of a fine old hero. The worst is he speaks very little French, and I have not learnt any German but what I pick up here and there, so we can't get on very well without an interpreter. I think his head and Platow's would make the finest subjects for beautiful old men. You have often read of General ——, of the Cossacks, who is in his own opinion a beauty and a great man *à bonnes fortunes*. In the opinion of others he is the greatest robber in existence, and the most disgusting *fanfaron* I ever saw!

What fun we should have if you were here with me, and how little *writing* answers to one's feelings. We received two days ago Lord Wellington's despatches, from Saint Pé. He is quite as much appreciated here as in England. . . . I must leave you to go and dress for dinner at the Chancellor Hardenberg's.

December 11

. . . The things you have sent to C.
Stewart for me are sure of being safe. . . .
Thank you for them a thousand times.
Muslin gowns are sure of being admired.
Cambric muslin and fine calico are thought
magnificent, and all kinds of English
jewellery run after, beyond what you can
conceive.   I never go out without having
my bracelets, rings, &c., looked at and
handed round. . . . I see Lord Byron has
published a new poem.   Pray send it
to me.

·   ·   ·   ·   ·   ·

Lady Burghersh to her Sister

Freiburg : December 15, 1813

My dearest Emily,—We arrived here
late last night, and performed the journey
with great speed, considering how full the
roads are, from Frankfurt here, with the
removal of the headquarters.   We left

Frankfurt at three o'clock on Sunday, and were here by nine yesterday evening (Tuesday). We came by Heidelberg, Darmstadt, and Carlsruhe, leaving Stuttgardt on our left, as we were anxious to get here soon on account of quarters, as this is a small town, and therefore the last comers will be but badly off. We are not near so well off as we were at Frankfurt, though we have got nearly the best quarters in the town, close to the Emperor's. The Austrians only are arrived as yet ; the Russians and Prussians are coming. Schwarzenberg came the day before us ; the Emperor Francis arrived at four o'clock to-day. He came into the town on horseback with his officers, &c., and was received with the greatest acclamations. All the windows were lined with women and children waving handkerchiefs, &c., &c., and throwing flowers. To-night the

.H

town is illuminated. The Emperor of
Russia has left Frankfurt, and will be here
in a few days ; the King of Prussia not
quite so soon.

I hear this is a pretty little town, but
I have not been out. It was very cold
to-day, and the town is all in confusion
with the marching in of the different regiments, scrambling for quarters, &c. I have
plenty of amusement from the windows.
Though we are here, I believe (*entre nous*)
we are just as far from coming to any
decision upon the plans to be pursued
as we were at Frankfurt. The Emperor
Francis and all his people are bent on one
plan ; the Emperor Alexander is directly
against it, and the King of Prussia dis-
approves of both! They are all equally
positive and obstinate, and as they cannot
act till one or the other gives way, the
time passes away, and *I* believe it will end

in our taking up winter quarters here or hereabouts. So much the better for me *individually*. As for the *cause*, the want of a Lord Wellington has been long felt, but Providence and the enthusiastic devotion of all ranks, and all nations, to the cause, will (as it has hitherto done) make up for that want.

I must tell you of an odd thing that happened to me on Monday night. I got out at the post-house about eleven at night while the horses were putting to. At the door we met Prince Metternich, who was travelling here also, and while B. was talking to him I got separated from him, the place being very full; and he, thinking I was gone into the room, went out with Metternich to see about the horses. I, not finding him or knowing where to go, opened the first door, which proved to be the kitchen, to the dire offence of an old woman, who immediately seized me by the arm, swearing in German as hard as she could jabber, and dragged me, notwithstanding my struggles, into a room, pushed me in and slapped the door upon me. I found myself in the middle of four Cossack officers who were eating their supper. I was a little scared, but one of the officers, having spoken in French, put me at ease directly, and I told them how I came there, and begged one of them to go out and look for *mon mari*, as I was afraid of going out alone, as I could not make myself understood. They were excessively civil, and another soon recognised me as *la dame Anglaise qui veut bien embellir notre quartier général*, and whom he had seen *à cheval dans les rues de Frankfort.* So by the time B. came in (which was not for a good while, as he had had a row to settle about the horses), he found me sitting with them in high conversation and the best friends possible. I never met with four civiller men. It is very lucky Madame Legoux was not with me, for, notwithstanding her courage in other respects, she is terribly afraid of *les militaires, et surtout, Miladi, ces vilains Cosaques.* She never gets out of the carriage when she can help it. We bought a very nice carriage at Offenbach, near Frankfurt, for her and Mr. Aubin[3] to travel in. The barouche they had before was a good deal shaken. Our own carriage is worth its weight in gold, for there has never been a nail out of its place since we left London, and it is so easy that even the bad roads hardly shake it. Now I have got to sleep quite soundly in it, and my cushion (Lord A.'s) is really the comfort of my life.

[3] Lord Burghersh's secretary.

I am all impatience to get your letters.
Dear Mama's account of herself delights
me.   I have never had a cold since I was
at Stralsund, but I find the climate here
to the full as changeable as it is in England.   We have had no snow to signify
yet, but very thick fogs the last three days,
which was unlucky, as the road from
Frankfurt here, along the banks of the
Rhine, is beautiful.   It is curious to feel
oneself within a few miles of France.
Who would have believed it last year ?

Lady Burghersh to her Mother

Freiburg : December 19, 1813

My   dearest   Mama,—I   have   just
learnt that Lord Aberdeen sends a courier
off to-night.   It is now late, but I will
write a line.   We have been in the midst
of such discussions, since my letter of last

Thursday to Emily, about the affair of Switzerland. Such plans, orders, and counter orders, indecisions, &c. ; but at length the Austrians have prevailed. I believe the troops have already marched, and will certainly enter Switzerland to-morrow, or at latest the day after. Schwarzenberg will not superintend the movement himself, as was at first intended, but will move the following day. We shall move with him. The next head-quarters are not quite fixed yet, but will probably be at a short distance from here —Lörrach or between Lörrach and Basle. Schwarzenberg has just been dining here ; there never was anything like his atten-tion and care of me. He has given me the best of his own *chasseurs*, mounted, to be always with my carriage and in my anteroom, and he will be of great service to me in moving and taking up quarters.

To-day the Bavarian army passed
through here; they are moving in the
same direction; they are fine troops. It
was interesting to see Wrede at the head
of them, who was supposed to be mortally
wounded at the battle of Hanau on
November 3 : indeed he was said to be
dead several times. They have not yet
been able to extract the ball, which is still
in the lower stomach, but he is well enough
to have been on horseback to-day, at the
head of his troops. The Emperor Francis
and all the Austrian officers were in the
street on horseback to see them. Alexander is not yet arrived. He was expected to-day, but did not come. I
suppose he will be here early to-morrow.
There has been a grand *réunion* at Carlsruhe ; the Queen of Sweden is there.

We are in a country which makes one
regret summer bitterly, for it must then be

Arthur, Marquis of Wellington?

Painted by J Heaphy at St Jean de Luz.
Dec.r 1813.

quite heavenly. The town is in a valley
surrounded by mountains, entirely covered
with vineyards, and the Rhine within
sight. There is a mountain just outside
the town from which the view is, even in
this season, quite enchanting. I am very
anxious to go to Schaffhausen to see the
falls of the Rhine, but as it is too far to
go and return in one day, I am afraid of
absenting myself while the headquarters
are on the point of moving. There are
two convents of nuns in this town, and
one of fat rosy friars. I am going to-
morrow to see the nuns. I saw the friars'
convent and chapel yesterday.

The Emperor of Austria is going to
send Lord Wellington the Grand Cross
of Maria Theresa, the first Austrian
order.

. . . . Christmas will be past and the
New Year begun before you get this

God bless you all through it, and grant we may meet before another begins. I shall think (too much, perhaps) of our Christmas dinner last year when we were all together; but such thoughts as those I don't and won't often indulge in; but thank God I am as well off as I am: so perfectly well in health and taken such good care of. I could wish I heard oftener from you all. It appears to me I get very few letters, but I am sure you write as often as you can. B. sends you a thousand loves. I never saw him better in my life. . . .

. . . I was in the act of sealing this letter when Prince Wenzel Liechtenstein came in to tell us three pieces of news, just arrived: the accession of Denmark and that of the King of Naples[4] to the good cause, and, what is to us better still,

---

[4] Murat, Napoleon's brother-in-law.

that Switzerland calls upon the allies and is ready to receive us with open arms. You may believe the joy it is to us, and to me in particular, to know that we shall meet with no opposition. Russia has also entirely waived all his objections to Austria's place, and all is now *d'accord*.

We all move to Lörrach to-morrow, and the next day to Basle. It is a glorious moment. What a change in the world in a few months! and must not all this soon bring the whole to an ending? God bless you! Denmark is a famous thing for our English shipping!

Lady Burghersh to her Father

Lörrach: December 22, 1813

My dearest Papa,—We have halted here at a small town, one (German) mile from Basle, to give time for the troops to

come up and pass the Rhine before we
proceed towards Berne. We left Freiburg Monday, that is to say the Austrians
under Schwarzenberg, for the Russians
and Prussians will not join us as yet; the
emperors and all the diplomatists remain
at Freiburg. We were obliged to come
all the way from Freiburg here with our
own horses, for every horse in the country
is taken up with the removal of waggons,
pontoons, &c. It is impossible without
seeing an army on a march to conceive
the state of the roads, completely covered
with artillery, waggons &c., and at night
the bivouacs extending all over the
country.

This town is little more than a village,
therefore you may imagine the state of it,
with all Schwarzenberg's headquarters in it.
Our quarter consists of one room, where
we eat, drink, and sleep. Yesterday 30,000

Austrian troops passed through the town, and crossed the Rhine at or about Rheinfeld, and to-day the whole Bavarian army, about 40,000 infantry and cavalry, with artillery, have gone through. They are remarkably fine troops, all young and in the best condition. It is impossible to say how wearing it is to see such an immense number of men march by ; they were from eight o'clock till past two, going by this house, without a moment's cessation. Wrede commands them. I wish you could see the women who follow the armies, particularly the Hungarians ; there is no doing justice to the horror of these monsters : they wear boots and other articles of dress exactly like men, and ride on men's saddles. Those who belong to the infantry, and therefore do not ride, carry baggage on their backs like packhorses ; it is quite extraordinary to see how they are loaded, and they do not seem to mind it the least. I have ridden to-day to a hill, a short distance from the town, which overlooks France. Though the day was extremely foggy, we could see quite plainly into the fortress of Huningue, even to see men working at the palisades, and could hear the firing of the small arms as distinctly as possible. Wrede and the Bavarians will immediately blockade Huningue : the Austrians, having passed the Rhine at different points between Schaffhausen and Rheinfeld, will assemble near Berne, where the headquarters will be transferred.

God knows what Buonaparte will do to oppose this force! If it should appear likely for fighting to begin, I should retire probably towards Zürich ; but I have plenty of safe places to choose, and I still hope I may not be obliged to leave the headquarters yet. Schwarzenberg will give me two Cossacks, as well as my chasseur, for my own body-guard, which is very respectable, besides B.'s dragoons.

We are very anxious for news from England, which we hope will also bring us news from Spain. . . . We have not yet seen our horses from England—they have been travelling all over the country after us, and are sure to arrive at a place two or three days after we have left it. . . . We have been obliged to buy a whole stud of both riding and carriage horses to carry us on. . . . We have the mildest possible weather. I hope we shall very soon be in Berne, which is a very good town, and get out of this nasty noisy place. . . .

I hope Emily's appetite does not fail her for mince pies : I wish I had a chance of eating any.

Lady Burghersh to her Sister

Lörrach : December 24, 1813

. . . We are still here. I believe Schwarzenberg wants to watch the pro-gress of the siege of Huningue, and to see if they will do anything from Strasburg, before he goes on. The troops have arrived at Berne and Neufchâtel. To be sure we are badly off enough here as to lodgings. Imagine one very dirty white-washed room with two casement windows, up a pair of stairs, in a small house in the principal street of a village in the middle of the mountains, which street is about three feet deep in mud, and quite filled up with the constant succession of baggage waggons, artillery, and troops passing through. In this one room we have our beds, we eat and we sit, and one goes out while the other dresses. There is just such another room, where Madame Legoux sleeps, and which is filled with the trunks, baggage, &c. Aubin and the servants sleep on straw in the kitchen and the stables! I don't mind it at all, and in this beautiful room I have always tea going on, and Schwarzenberg, Liechten-stein, and most of the staff generally come in and drink tea.

We hear the firing at Huningue quite distinctly; the siege is not begun, but there is a constant popping kept up at the advanced posts of the Bavarians. To-day we rode up close to Basle (but did not go into it); there was a great deal of firing at Huningue while we were there, and we could even hear the balls whizzing through the air. The bombardment they say will begin to-night. Schwarzenberg is going to have a hut made on the hill behind this

town, which overlooks Huningue, for me
to see it from.   They do not expect it to
hold out above two or three days.

.   .   .   .   .   .

I regret every day that we are in this
beautiful country at such a season.   We
have had such thick fogs that we have
never seen the tops of the mountains, and
when we get half way up them, we can't
see the valleys ; but we must not complain,
for we have wonderfully mild weather and
no snow.   I ride a great deal, and my
horse is perfection, and the greatest beauty
you ever saw !   He is iron-grey—I should
like to put you on him !   All the people
about here have *goîtres*, which are very
disgusting, but the women are pretty.
They all wear their hair plaited down their
backs with ribbon ; but I have not seen
any of the pretty Swiss dresses yet. . . .

December 26

I could not help thinking of home all yesterday—Christmas Day—and of last year, when we all dined together in Savile Row.[5] Don't you remember it was quite an event for neither Mary[6] nor me to be in Staffordshire or at Apethorpe?

I spent my Christmas Day in taking a ride in France. We went through Basle, and along the road opposite Huningue. The French were firing all the time —like fools to waste their balls! It was the finest day I ever saw; the first clear frost we have had; we could see them in the fortress quite plain. We met upon the road a French soldier who had deserted from Metz, and just walked quietly on in his uniform without molestation. He told us there were 30,000 men in

---

[5] Mr. Wellesley Pole's house in London.
[6] Her eldest sister, wife of Sir Charles Bagot.

Metz. The Austrians have occupied the town of Belfort successfully. The bombardment of Huningue has not begun—they cannot get their cannon up as soon as they expected.

We get papers from Paris here in three days! They seem in a terrible fright. The last mentioned an idea of Buonaparte going directly to Brussels. How differently we stand now to what we did last year, when I was so angry at Tunbridge at Charles's[7] croaking.

Lady Burghersh to her Mother

Lörrach: December 28

.   .   .   .   .   .

A thousand thanks, my own dearest Mama, for your two very dear letters. . . . The bare idea of your coming over in the summer makes my heart jump, but I will hope even better that our work may be

[7] Sir Charles Bagot.

ended, and that we may be together in dear England, for no place is like that, after all. I am well convinced that had a Lord Wellington existed here the work would have been ended two months ago, and we should not have spent so many idle weeks at Frankfurt, but time lost can never be redeemed; and if too many *good* cooks spoil the broth, how good must the broth be which is not spoiled by so many *bad* ones!

All our plans here are again altered. I do not believe the headquarters will go to Berne at all. 90,000 of the troops are already arrived there, but I believe our headquarters will remain here, at least till we see what Buonaparte means to do against us. The two Emperors and the King of Prussia, with all the diplomatists and the Russian and Prussian guards, remain at Freiburg ; Barclay de Tolly and his army will be up with us in a few days, and Wittgenstein is just behind us. The bombardment of Huningue again put off till to-morrow ; and so we go on. For myself, I shall be sorry not to see Berne, and, being on the confines, not to go further into Switzerland.

We went yesterday to Basle to a great dinner given by Sir R. Wilson to all the Austrian and Bavarian officers, previous to his going to the Italian army, for which he takes his departure in two days. We stayed all night at Basle, and came back to-day. It is a very pretty, clean, cheerful town, and seems so delightful after this, that we have taken quarters there, and mean to be backwards and forwards, and remain there when there is nothing going on here, as it is not more than three or four English miles from here.

We were delighted on our return

here to see Tibbets and Samuel [8] grin-
ning at the door, having just arrived with
the horses. The poor men thought they
should never catch us, I believe! The
horses are well, only a little lame, which is
not to be wondered at considering the
immensely long journey and the bad roads.
James [9] is an excellent servant in out-
landish parts, and can speak German very
tolerably already. Our *maître d'hôtel* [1]
curls his hair, wears earrings and rouge,
lisps, and walks on tiptoe, for which sundry
reasons we should be glad to pick up
another ; but, what is most essential, we
have got an excellent cook, and a very
careful, good coachman. Our family is
pretty considerable, having (dragoons and
all) nineteen souls and twenty horses to
feed and carry about ! . . .

[8] Their grooms.   [9] The English footman.
[1] Engaged at Frankfurt.

Schwarzenberg is remarkably good-humoured and perfectly gentlemanlike. He reminds me of a Legge, particularly of the Admiral Arthur Legge, that sort of good-looking, jolly face. I don't much like what I have seen of the Bavarian officers, of whom we had a good lot at dinner yesterday. They are such complete Frenchmen, with short-waisted uniforms all covered with gold and silver. In short, of all the different nations I have seen, I think the Prussians are the best. I think when I return I shall amuse you with many things one can't write, or do justice to in writing. I am wonderfully well in body and mind, quite strong, much fatter, and I have not had an inkling of a cold since I left Sweden. I am surprised at it myself, but much more surprised to find myself always contented and gay, without anxieties or fears on any one subject, not minding noise, stink, or dirt in the least, and quite bold on horseback and amongst men and soldiers, even Cossacks, who are the greatest thieves in the world! I believe God has changed me inside and out expressly for this journey, and for that one cannot be sufficiently thankful. . . .

As to Lord Wellington, I should not wonder if we were to meet before either of us sees England again.

.   .   .   .   .   .

Lady Burghersh to her Father

Basle : January 3, 1814

My dearest Papa,— . . . We moved from Lörrach here two days ago, to my great joy, for we left a most horrible hole, and are now in excellent quarters in a very nice town. I don't believe there can be a more beautiful view in the world than from my windows, even at this time of year : close to the banks of the Rhine, which is as clear as glass, the hills of Baden cultivated up to the top, and beyond the mountains of Switzerland covered with snow ; behind us France.

Huningue is just opposite. The bombardment began at twelve at night on the 31st, to usher in the new year, and has continued every night since. From my bed I see the shot and the shells bursting. The noise at first prevented sleep, but now I am so used to it that it does not disturb me at all. They think it will hold out some time ; they are strong and well provisioned. This day Schwarzenberg moves his headquarters into France, to Altkirch, a small place on the road to Belfort, about seven leagues from hence. I do not mean to follow for a day or two till they have got my quarters and are a little settled, for I had a lesson at Lörrach of scrambling in the same day with them all.

The Russian army (Barclay de Tolly) come to-day into Lörrach, the Emperors and King, &c., will soon come on and join us, whenever we can get to a place big enough to contain us all, which I shall be glad of, for the more the merrier in this kind of life. It is, however, a most interesting existence, and will furnish me with recollections for the rest of my life. As my room is the *point de réunion* and my English tea is a great luxury, so all the great and little people meet every evening, and all the most interesting discussions pass at my tea-table, and all the different reports from different quarters which are brought to the different generals make it always agreeable. Here we have the addition of the Swiss deputies and General Watteville, with the Bavarians; as they know I am always glad to see them every evening, they come in and out, and I know in that way all that goes on.

We hear from France that Lord Wellington gained a great victory on the 14th close to Bayonne;[2] we are of course very anxious for the details. Here we do not expect anything decisive till after the 13th or 14th, as we have no news of the French collecting as yet. A few days ago we believed Buonaparte to be gone to Brussels, but the last accounts from Paris speak of his being still there. I send you a portrait of him, said to be like.

.   .   .   .   .   .

[2] At St. Jean de Luz.

Lady Burghersh to her Mother

Basle : January 10

My dearest Mama,— . . . Last night I received the long-delayed parcel. I can't describe to you what the sight of your silver gown made me feel. It brought your own self so before me. . . . I was so provoked, the sea-water had gone over it, and so it did not smell of violets, which would have put me quite beside myself. . . .

. . . I have been here alone since Friday. I submitted to the opinion that I had better not attend the advanced posts into France till a little time has passed, though hitherto the French people have received the allies admirably, and no French army is to be heard of! Schwarzenberg moved his headquarters first to

Altkirch, then to Montbelliard, where B.
joined them, and to-day to Vesoul, in-
tending to push on directly to Langres.
Everywhere the inhabitants have received
them with delight, as they have done
Blücher in the direction of Metz. Schwarzenberg wished me to come to Montbelliard and return here when they went on.
I meant to have done so, but, on finding
the two Emperors and King were coming
to fix their headquarters here, I determined to remain here at once; for fear of
losing my quarters, which were sure to be
snatched up if I had left them a moment.
As it was, I had difficulty enough in keeping them. I am not at all uneasy at remaining here as I am so near, and B. will
be constantly backwards and forwards as
the Emperors, &c. come here, and whenever they move on I can go with them in
all safety. B. will certainly be here in a

few days to meet Lord Castlereagh, who is expected daily. The Emperor Francis comes to-morrow ; the next day Alexander will cross the Rhine and enter the town at the head of his army, which will be a fine thing to see. The same day the King of Prussia, with all the ministers &c. come. . . . I am very happy they are all coming, as, since B. went, I have been here without one human being in or near the town whose face I knew.

This evening Prince Radziwill arrived and came to me. I was quite overjoyed to see an acquaintance, for I found it very lonely after being used to see so many people. I am told my tea-parties were thought delightful by *ces messieurs du quartier général*, and that Schwarzenberg, &c., say they don't know how they shall pass their lives now I am left behind !

The siege goes on very slowly and

very tamely; there is but little firing. Is it not most wonderful that the allies should now be in so many different points in France, and that we cannot hear of any French army whatever collecting any-where? The accounts given by spies, deserters, and prisoners all agree that there is no army, at least none to be seen. I would bet a great deal we have an immediate peace. From all I hear (and I hear everything that goes on, every report and every opinion) I have not the least doubt in my own mind that the thing is over. As myself, Priscilla, you may believe I have no little joy; but as *a soldier*, I must think it a pity to have had the power, and not to have crushed that wretch! . . .

. . . The snow has set in here, and I am in hopes of some *traineau* parties, which I am anxious to see. I am happy to be so well and comfortably lodged in the cold weather, and to have got out of that horrid Lörrach. As to catching cold, I have forgotten how.

We hear of Lord Wellington's victories through France only, and that in an uncertain way, but I hope we shall soon establish a line of communication with him through the south of France. Platow and his Cossacks are at Nancy.

.   .   .   .   .   .

Lady Burghersh to her Sister

Basle : January 14, 1814

The imperial headquarters are all arrived here, but Lord Castlereagh is not yet come, nor is B. returned. I got a letter from him yesterday : they are at Vesoul, getting on to Langres. Received everywhere with open arms, and the

K

people supply them with everything they want. Besançon is invested, and the people of the town have refused to obey Buonaparte's order to form a guard for the town. In short, everything goes on brilliantly. There is an idea that there are some French troops in Langres, but they must be very weak. Yesterday (being the Russian New Year's Day) the Russian army with a great part of the Prussian, all in their best accoutrements, passed the Rhine, and defiled in the town before the two Emperors and King, &c. It is impossible to see a finer sight or a more interesting one, than to see these men and recollect what they have done since last year, and now in such perfect order, the horses in such excellent condition, and the men (especially the Russians) so clean. Soldiers will tell you it is ridiculous, but there is a *recherche* and *coquetterie* in most of the Russian regiments, which make them a sight too magnificent to be described! The extreme care and cleanliness of their dress is quite beautiful. The Cossacks of the guard and the Emperor's footguard are all picked men, the handsomest of the empire. The latter are all gigantic; they are composed of the tallest men to be found in Russia; their coats are all padded to stuff out their chests and widen their shoulders, and therefore they really look like statues for fine make. Don't think I exaggerate, for everyone raves of them. The Prussians are fine troops, and probably much the better, as troops; but one cannot look at them after the Russians. The town was illuminated last night. The Emperors have some idea of moving to Montbelliard in a few days, but I rather think they will stay and negotiate here.

All the ambassadors are arrived, including C. Stewart with young James. . . . It was very lucky for me they did arrive, for the people of the house I am in are so enraged at not having the King instead of me, that they have tried *l'impossible* to get me out, and, finding nothing would stir me, they have flown to open war, and such hostilities rage between masters and servants that I have had no end of rows, and at last had to call in the authority of le Général Stewart, backed by the *quartierants*, to settle them. Yesterday evening, while I was quietly reading ' Corinne,' the woman of the house flew in to say she would turn my *chasseur* out of the house because he spit in the kitchen ; and she was followed by William, the English footman I got at Frankfort, in tears, declaring he should lose his senses because they insulted his country ! I could not help it, but I burst out laughing and laughed till I cried—don't you know the sort of thing? But finding, with all my impudence, I could not 'jaw' sufficiently, I this morning called in the aid of Mr. James, who has, I believe, settled them.

.   .   .   .   .   .

Lady Burghersh to ——————

Basle : January 20, 1814

. . . We are all on the wing for Vesoul! Our Emperor goes to-morrow or Saturday; the King is gone; I go on Sunday. I let them all go on first to secure horses, quarters, &c., &c. for me. Schwarzenberg's headquarters are at Langres. I was woke this morning by a note from Metternich announcing that Langres was ready to be laid *à vos jolis pieds*, and without the least resistance. I

am so very happy to-day, so much easier
than I have been for many days, till it was
decided if they would get hold of so strong
a place as Langres without at least as
much resistance as Mortier's small force
could oppose. Now negotiations will begin
and peace be signed before the French
have an opportunity of making a stand;
so everyone thinks.   This evening one of
Schwarzenberg's aides-de-camp arrived
with the keys of Langres to lay before the
Emperor.   He has just been with me and
brought me letters from Burghersh. They
established themselves at Langres on the
18th.   Our headquarters go at first only
to Vesoul, but B. will certainly come there
to see Lord Castlereagh, and Schwarzenberg sent me word to-night that all was
perfectly safe, and that I should be quite
as well at Langres as here.

Lord Castlereagh arrived the day

before yesterday, and came here to tea
last night with Mr. Robinson and Mr.
Planta, the only two he has brought with
him.   Lady Castlereagh wanted very
much to come on, but he will not let her
leave Holland. . . .

I never was more surprised than to
hear of William's [3] coming.   It will make
me very happy to see him, for if I
feel quite to love anything English
I see, what must it be to see one of
my own   I am in great impatience to
move on from hence ; it is now nearly a
fortnight since B. went, and then we were
certain of meeting in a few days. . . .

I am sure you will be pleased to
hear how very much Lord Castlereagh
approves of B.   He says his despatches
astonished everyone in England, from

[3] Her brother ; he did not however carry out his intention.

the talent and cleverness they showed, and that the last in particular, he thinks, is not to be beat by anything of the sort he ever received, and he seems quite pleased with his whole conduct. . . .

I have hardly had time to read Arthur's[4] despatch, as the papers only came just before dinner, and the courier for England going off to-morrow morning early, I am anxious to get my letters done. There appears to be a great list of killed. I believe we shall meet him at Paris![5] Only imagine that. The Emperor Alexander has set his heart on going there; the Austrians, on the contrary, wish to negotiate and end it all here. Prussia is very quiet and ready for either, I believe.

[4] Duke of Wellington : always called Arthur in his family then. The despatch was that from St. Jean de Luz, describing the passage of the Nive.
[5] They did.

It is certainly most entertaining and
extraordinary to follow all the workings,
the squabbles, the different views and
ends, &c. I shall have enough to talk
and think about all my life. How you
would laugh to see me (the helpless creature I was in England) by myself, arranging my journey, my money matters, ex-
change, &c., the horses, dragoons—everything on my shoulders, and really it gives
me no sort of trouble or anxiety. E.
amuses me talking of her 'terribly
tedious' journey to Brighton of thirteen
hours. We are always from eighteen to
twenty-two hours in the carriage, and that
for days together. I shall be more going
to Vesoul, for I do not mean to stop on
the road, but go through at once, as I do
not like the idea of sleeping at any sort
of French inn by myself, and I mean
my carriage to follow Metternich's, as he

remains till Sunday. Our mild weather is come back and is delightful. . . .

I believe I told you that at Frankfurt there was a great deal of Brussels lace to be had . . . but here there is neither lace nor anything else to be had; I believe I shall have to wait to get it at Paris! I wonder if we shall fall in with Edward Paget.[6] I went into a shop here the other day to look at some Lyons silks . . . and the man told me he had sold some a few months back at Moulins to *un de vos compatriotes, Milord Beverley et d'autres Anglais*. Belfort and Huningue remain in the same state, blockaded but no firing. Blücher is at Nancy.

·   ·   ·   ·   ·   ·

[6] Brother of Lord Anglesey, who had been one of the English detained prisoners in France after the rupture of the Peace of Amiens.

Lady Burghersh to her Mother

Basle : January 22

My dearest Mama,—Count Merveldt has just sent to say he sets off tomorrow for England, so I must write you a line by him, though I am in all the hurry and worry of departure and bothered out of my wits about passports, billets, &c. I set off at twelve o'clock to-night, following Metternich's carriage ; we shall get to Vesoul to-morrow evening, and if I do not find B. there, he will certainly be there in a day or two. Yesterday Schwarzenberg sent one of his orderlies to me from Langres to tell me there was now no reason at all against my going on to his headquarters if I chose, and that the sooner I arrived the better ; but as I knew B. does not like me to advance beyond the Emperors, I shall stay with them, at least till he comes to me. Indeed it is most likely they will all go soon to Langres. It is a secret, but I am so happy at it.

The armies will not advance or attempt anything more till peace has been offered, and I believe we may be pretty sure that will not be rejected, so I verily think our campaign is over. Think of our occupying Langres, Nancy, Dijon, without firing a shot, and the Prince Royal of Würtemberg has got his advance at Chaumont! The French people everywhere delighted to see them. . . .

Lady Burghersh to her Sister

Langres : January 26

You will be surprised to see this letter so soon, dated from this place. . . .

I left Basle on Sunday at two o'clock,
instead of the night before, as Prince
Metternich could not get his business over
before. I dined with him at one o'clock,
and we set out together. However, as he
had the Emperor's good horses and I had
wretched post horses, I soon lost sight
of him, and he got to Vesoul many hours
before me. I did not stop at all between
Basle and Vesoul, and was thirty-one
hours in the carriage through the coldest
night I ever felt, and indeed it is reckoned
extraordinarily cold even for this part of
the world. At Vesoul, unexpectedly, and
to my great joy, I found Burghersh, who
on hearing I had left Basle came from
here to meet me there, and as the Emperors' headquarters were all moving on
here, we proceeded and arrived here to-
day. As Schwarzenberg is here also, we
are all united for the moment. Schwarz-

enberg intends moving his headquarters
to Chaumont. I have not settled whether
I shall go there with him, or remain here.
I am not the least tired with my journey,
nor have I suffered from the cold at all.
So here we are, far advanced in France,
and I can only say that after all the places
I have been in, I never met with hospitality and cordiality till here ; at every
place every individual has received us
with the most genuine delight, and though
the country is really almost exhausted
from the passage of so large an army
without any magazines, the people give us
everything they have and show an eagerness to do their utmost which is delightful.
They all talk of Buonaparte exactly in the
same manner, as a monster whom they
detest, and then, with the levity and gaiety
of the French, in the midst of their com-
plaints at all they suffer under him, the

loss of their children by the conscription, the ruin of commerce, &c., they mix it up with jokes and quizzes of him and *les gentillesses du Roi de Rome.* They say that since his defeats *Napoléon est toujours soûl.* They say that for four years the war in Spain has been the subject of universal execration. It is impossible to conceive a greater contrast than coming out of Germany into France, where the sort of manner in which the people jabber and chatter, though it is sometimes amusing, at times is also too provoking. I am a great sight here, both as an Englishwoman and as the only woman with the armies, and they all run to look at *la princesse anglaise,* as I am always called. I suppose the headquarters will remain here as long as there remains anything to eat or any forage in the country—which cannot be long, I take it.

Blücher's army is nearly concentrated with ours, and Platow is at Bar-sur-Aube, which is, if I remember right, quite close to Mademoiselle's [7] Ricey. She need have no anxiety about her family, for no one could conceive that a large army was in an enemy's country; on the contrary, the people are much more friendly than they were in their own land. We are within twenty-four hours' journey of Paris, and as yet we hear of no preparations to check us, the small force under Mortier, which evacuated this place on the 17th, leaving twelve pieces of cannon, have retired to Troyes. Peace will probably be signed in a very short time. The treating begins immediately, and no one has yet expressed a doubt of the issue.

Lord Castlereagh has pleased very

[7] Her old governess, Mlle. Quenday, an *émigrée*, who had brought her and her sisters up.

much here. They say he has *une fort belle physiognomie*, and seem to like him extremely. His placidity of course never ruffles. I hear that Lord Beverley and his son [8] are still at Moulins, but E. Paget has been some time at Paris. Two Englishmen, who had been prisoners and came from Moulins to headquarters, brought this intelligence. . . .

January 27

I continue this to-night, being just returned from a great dinner at Lord Aberdeen's, where I had a long *codger* with Schwarzenberg, and, as he assures me I shall find no sort of difficulty at Chaumont, I have decided to move there with B. to-morrow, and I am not a little happy to go on with him instead of staying at these headquarters. I do not think the

---

[8] English prisoners.

Emperors will continue here many days. The Emperor Alexander is all impatience to advance, and he generally gets his own way.

There was a very brilliant affair, two days ago, between Mortier and the Prince Royal of Würtemberg, near Bar-sur-Aube, where the latter ' drubbed' him and killed 2,000 men ; the Austrians lost about 800 killed and wounded. I have been walking about this town to-day, which seems a good one, but there is nothing to be seen, as the people have all shut up their shops for fear of being plundered. They are terribly afraid of the Cossacks, and not without reason, for robbing and plundering is their system among friends as well as enemies.

Lady Burghersh to her Mother

Chaumont : February 3
Thursday morning

My dearest Mama,—I feel this morning as if I had had a hundredweight
taken off my heart after all I have suffered
of anxiety since the 28th—the day we
heard of Buonaparte's having taken the
command of his army, and attacked
Blücher, who beat him as usual (fine old
fellow!) at Brienne. Schwarzenberg, upon
this, determined to collect his force and
attack him in his position at Dieuville, a
few leagues from this place. As he could
not, however, get Wrede's corps up the
next day, the attack was determined upon
for Tuesday, the day before yesterday,
when they all set out from hence early in
the morning. However, we got a report

L 2

that in the night Buonaparte had retired, and that he would not come to action, which appeared so probable, and was so generally believed, that many officers and persons, not under orders, thought there would be no fighting, and did not follow Schwarzenberg. . . . I heard nothing all day and went to bed quite easy and secure that they had done nothing, but was woke in the night by the arrival of a courier to bring me the account of the battle of which you will have the details.

It appears Buonaparte's retiring was a feint, and his force much stronger than we supposed. Mortier having joined him, he had between 70,000 and 80,000 men. I hear they fought admirably. Buonaparte charged himself at the head of his young guards three times, and was three times repulsed. We have taken fifty-six pieces of cannon ; the battle lasted from twelve till dark.   B. wrote to me from Bar-sur-Aube, where the headquarters were after the battle,[9] and they were preparing to re-attack the enemy the next morning (yester-day) with great reinforcements.   Conceive my state of mind through the day, for though I knew B. ought not to be exposed, yet it was impossible not to suffer the greatest anxiety in every way, and inde-pendently of him, to know every soul with whom one is living intimately, engaged ! Besides that, the poor people in the house, terrified out of their wits for the event of the battle, running to me every moment and telling me they heard the cannon from the gates of the town (a lie).   About eleven at night the door opened and Charles Stewart entered, saying ' All is well !'   It is im-possible to describe the sort of joy and relief I felt.   He then told me I might

[9] Of La Rothière and Brienne.

have saved my fears, as Buonaparte would not stay to be beat again, and has run for it towards Paris. The armies follow him up, and to-day Schwarzenberg's headquarters are at Vaudœuvres. The Emperor of Russia and King of Prussia arrived in the rear during the battle of Tuesday. Of course, from their advancing, B. could not return here, so I am again left without him.

The Emperor of Austria has not yet left Langres. Till I hear where he goes I can't decide any plans. I cannot of course be with Schwarzenberg while he is in pursuit of the enemy. The Congress opens at Châtillon this day, twelve leagues from hence. Caulaincourt for France ; a Commission of three (consisting of Lord Cathcart, Lord Aberdeen, and Sir Charles Stewart) for England ; Count Stadion for Austria ; Count Rasumoffsky for Russia. Lord Castlereagh is there, though he does not treat. While writing this, I have just heard the Emperor of Austria comes here to-day, so I shall not move.

I must tell you a speech so like a Frenchman which was made the day of the battle at Brienne. One of the Prussian officers entered into conversation with a French soldier at the outposts, and said to him, ' *Savez-vous que le Roi de Naples et le Danemarc se sont réunis aux alliés ?* ' The soldier answered, ' *Cela n'est pas vrai.*' The officer continued, ' *Pourquoi continuez-vous la guerre ? vous la faites pour un tyran qui cause le malheur de l'univers.*' ' *Cela est vrai,*' answered the Frenchman. And so it ended.

The town of Brienne was burnt. There is a very fine château there, which contained a famous museum of stuffed birds, shells, and natural curiosities. It has been, of course, destroyed and pulled to pieces, but from the *débris* they sent me a few shells as trophies, which are and will be memorable.

I wish you could see that delightful, fine old Blücher. At seventy-two years old he tires out all his young aides-de-camp and officers, and is equally alert in mind and body. He calls Burghersh the 'lord of the *schöne Frau*,' i.e. the pretty wife! The Russians are very jealous of his having had the first battle in France. Platow is on at Sens. The Empress of Russia is now at Berlin on her way to Carlsruhe to see her family. I should like to see her. They say she is quite an angel. . . .

I hope you will have the charity to send me the new poem which I see Lord Byron is publishing,[1] and also Miss Burney's (or rather, I believe, Madame

---

[1] *The Corsair.*

d'Arblay's) new novel.[2] I have not a book to read, and one can get nothing in these towns, as all the people shut up their shops for fear of pillage. To-day is B.'s birthday. It is rather hard to be away from him, but it cannot last long. If Châtillon does not produce peace in a few days we shall be at Paris, I suppose.

We have very severe weather and a deep snow, which seems to intend lasting the year. It is hard for the poor soldiers, but the armies are in most excellent condition, and there are very few sick. Schwarzenberg has 190,000 men under his orders here, but there were not above 80,000 engaged. The loss was severe : I don't know what. C. Stewart says he left the dead yesterday piled up in heaps. . . .

.　　.　　.　　.

[2] *The Wanderer.*

Lady Burghersh to her Sister Emily

Bar-sur-Aube : February 6, 1814

My dearest E.,— . . . I must now tell you all my history since I wrote to Mama on the 3rd, just after the battle of Brienne.

The Emperor Francis was then behind me at Langres, and I expected he would come to Chaumont to fix for some days. Depending upon this, I was under no uneasiness at being there alone, knowing myself between him and the rear guard and the other Emperor &c. with the army. I sent all the horses away with B. and his baggage waggon, knowing that Prince Metternich would take care to give me requisition horses when he and the Emperor moved on. My whole dependence was on them. Conceive, therefore, my sensations on Friday morning when

I heard that the Emperor, Metternich &c. &c., in short the whole court, had gone by in the night and proceeded to Bar-sur-Aube! So I found myself entirely alone in the town, not even a garrison left, not one soul I could apply to, no order for horses, no passport, no billet for quarters, even if I could get off, and the wounded from the battle coming in by cartfuls to make the *séjour* agreeable.

For the first time in all my difficulties I was completely discouraged, and sat for an hour quite bewildered; add to all, I had no news whatever of B. since the battle, and no one knew what the armies were doing, and that the *chasseur* whom Prince Schwarzenberg had given me, and whom I depended upon, had been put in arrest for some regimental fault; and I had that morning got a strange one. I think no one ought ever to have any anxiety about me after getting myself, by myself, out of such a situation.

After despairing for an hour I began to think that I must do something for myself, and that with five senses and money I might do much, so I set about the means of getting on, for the rear of an army is, for many reasons, much the worst place to be in. I sent to the mayor of the town, and after every sort of difficulty, rowing, begging, threatening, and forcing, I got four wretched requisition horses; but the driver ran off, and after waiting from nine in the morning till two, I got hold of a one-armed man whom I made drive, and set off boldly, having sent a servant on here to tell Prince Metternich to get me quarters.

I arrived safe and sound last night, and found to my joy the Emperor Francis's headquarters still here; I met

also on the road a messenger from B.,
who is at Bar-sur-Seine, and who was in
a terrible taking when he heard the Emperor had arrived here without me.

We are now in great anxiety to-day.
Buonaparte is at Troyes, and as he has a
good position, it is expected he will try
to make a stand and probably attack the
allies. Till this is decided, the Emperor's
plans are not fixed. B. writes me word
to arrange my plans with Metternich, that
is, if he thinks I had better not stick to
the Emperor, I must go to Châtillon,
where the congress is, and all the English,
and where I should know all that goes on.
I had much rather stay with the Emperor
if I can, but it is a good thing to have
such a retreat as Châtillon, and I shall be
guided by Metternich. I expect him here
every moment and shall not close this till
I am decided. Much of the future move-

ments will depend on the turn things take at Châtillon. I expect every hour a courier from them with a report of the first conference with Caulaincourt, the French Plenipotentiary, which took place yesterday. B. is only a few miles on. It is hard I cannot get to him or he to me. Alexander and the King of Prussia are both gone on ; it is only old Franz who stays behind.

It is certainly the most interesting moment which perhaps the annals of the world afford. Every hour may produce great events. In the midst of all I am well, quiet and happy after some moments of anxiety are passed. It is a dreadful sight to see the wounded coming in after a battle ; we met quantities on the road. Our loss has been very severe, I fear, but the Würtembergers and Prussians suffered most.

We have a magnificent army assembled here, but it will ruin the country, which is poor and already exhausted. I hope we shall soon have Troyes, where we may be all together. Pray tell Mademoiselle [3] that I happened to hear the day I left Chaumont of a M. Duval, who was going that day to Ricey Haut, and that I desired him to call at her mother's or brother's, and say that *une des élèves de sa fille Françoise* had been at Chaumont, and that the last accounts I had she was well and happy in England. I was afraid of writing myself, not knowing who or what may be in Ricey.

I am sorry, my dear, I have no chance of getting any more Swedish gloves. It is difficult to get them even in Sweden, but I will tell you what I will do. A young Swede made me a present of two

[3] Her old French *bonne*.

pair of very rare gloves, which can only be made in one village in Sweden, from the water of a particular spring. They are the same sort as the others, only a great deal softer and finer, and you shall have them, but I cannot send them now, as they are in a trunk, and I must not undo a trunk now, as I am obliged to be ready to start at a moment's notice.

.   .   .   .   .   .

How can you ask who is Prince Metternich? I thought everybody knew the fame of so great a person, who is, and has been for years, the mainspring of all that passes on the Continent. He is the Emperor of Austria's prime minister, and reckoned the best and deepest diplomatist going. He is wonderfully clever, and manages all the emperors, kings, and ministers, turning them round his little finger, and they are all afraid of him. . . .

He is uncommonly agreeable and good
looking. . . . The two other prime
ministers are Nesselrode (the Emperor
of Russia's), a little, sharp, cunning, ugly
fellow ; and the King of Prussia's minister,
Hardenberg, who is like Sir W. Far-
quhar, and gives one the idea of just such
a good, worthy old man. He has *de quoi*
to be very agreeable, but is so terribly
deaf that one must roar to him, which
prevents all conversation. . . .

. . . A courier is arrived from
Schwarzenberg. Instead of attacking,
Buonaparte is retiring upon Nogent, behind Troyes : so far good. Metternich
says I have no reason to go to Châtillon,
but had better on all accounts remain with
the Emperor, who will stay here over to-
morrow, and then talks of moving his
headquarters to Ricey. . . . The Emperor
is ill to-day, and has got *une terrible*

M

migraine. The fact is the poor man is completely miserable about his daughter, whom he loves very much. She is not much liked here in France ; they say she is so very proud.[4] . . .

. . . . . .

Lady Burghersh to her Mother

Troyes : February 8, 1814

My dearest Mama,—You will be glad to hear I have again rejoined B., having arrived here this day. When I wrote to Emily two days ago from Bar-sur-Aube, our headquarters (that is, the Emperor's) were to move the next day to Ricey ; but having that day received intelligence of Troyes' surrender

[4] The Empress Marie Louise. Some years later Lady Burghersh became very intimate with her in Italy, and found out then that the coldness, which was taken for pride in France, was in truth extreme shyness.

without resistance, Ricey was given up,
and this morning the Emperor, Prince
Metternich, and I all set out at the same
time for this place, where B. came with
Schwarzenberg last night, and so I have
the happiness to be with him again.
Finding a courier going off to-night, I
cannot resist writing a few lines, though
I cannot tell you much, being but just
arrived. This seems a large, ugly, dirty
town, and is brim full, having the two
Emperors', the King's, and Schwarzenberg's headquarters—all united. I fear
the latter will move on in a couple of
days, but our old Emperor will remain
here. I shall either stay with him or go
to Châtillon, as circumstances may direct.
I am very happy to have managed my
matters so well as to arrive here and catch
B. flying, at least for a day or two.
Though we have been but a few leagues

from each other, we have been dodging about, so that he knew so little where I was gone to that he set off two days ago and went to Châtillon, thinking to find me there, whilst I was at Bar-sur-Aube. He was delighted to see me arrive here safe and sound. The country presents a most woeful spectacle, and the remains of the battle reminded me of the objects on the line of retreat in Germany. The poor inhabitants suffer greatly, for the country is completely exhausted, and there literally is hardly sustenance left in the places we have passed through ; besides, notwithstanding all the pains which the commanders take to prevent pillage, it is impossible to keep the troops from excesses of all kinds, to the utter ruin of the unfortunate people. Indeed, the scenes of misery one is witness to are enough to break one's heart, and the worst is, there is no remedy. Nothing can be more humane or well-intentioned than all the sovereigns, Schwarzenberg, and, indeed, the whole set of those in command ; but it is of no avail, particularly with the Cossacks, who know no law. Indeed, I am sick of war and all its horrors, and long to get away from such scenes.

It is odd we should have been so very near going to Mademoiselle's home! I hear it is a very pretty town. If I go from hence to Châtillon (which I shall not if I can help it), I shall pass very near it, and certainly, if I find it practicable, I will go there. The negotiations at Châtillon seem likely to *trainer*. . . .

.   .   .   .   .   .

Lady Burghersh to her ——

Troyes : February 12, 1814

. . . We are all still here. The departure of the Austrians and Russians was fixed for to-day, but owing to some (I fear foolish) business of a Russian corps under Blücher, the intended manœuvre is altered, and they will not move till the day after to-morrow. When they do move, I have consented to go to Châtillon. B. is uneasy at the idea of my advancing further now the operations have become so very active, and as there must soon be something very decided. It is all very smooth as long as we go on victoriously ; but if we should receive the least check, and be obliged to make a retrograde movement, I should certainly then be exposed to difficulty. God forbid such a thing should happen, for a retreat through this country would be really terrific ; it is now completely drained.

I am very sorry to leave B., and very sorry to leave the armies, which interest me so much ; but I own I shall rejoice to get from the sight of such misery as we witness at every step. It makes one's heart bleed, and I really do not see how these wretched inhabitants are to escape starvation after we leave them. I never saw so filthy a town as this, and the number of beggars far surpasses that of Dublin : all women and children, for of spare men there are none ; but the former follow you about the streets in herds of twenty and thirty together. If you give money to one, the rest all fall on her, and then begins a regular fight. I live in the great street, and spend the day at the window, from whence I have the pleasure of seeing four or five battles every day.

There is a most magnificent cathedral here, built in the time of St. Louis, and full of the most beautiful painted glass I ever saw. There is also a very good theatre, where I have been every night, and where they give little operas and vaudevilles very well, getting the Russian musicians to make up the orchestra. One night there were two women in the gallery ; the other nights I have been the only female in the boxes, pit, or gallery, the house being entirely filled with the army. The King of Prussia and his two uncommonly nice boys[5] go every night. . . .

One may form some idea of the wretchedness of France by this town,

[5] Frederick William IV. and the Emperor William I.

which is one of the principal ones, and
which is really more vile than Deptford,
and such multitudes of miserable-looking
women ; one never sees a young man,
and I am particularly struck with not seeing any babies whatever. Last night Jules
and Armand de Polignac arrived here, to
the great joy of everyone, having made
their escape from Paris on the very day
on which they were destined to be moved
with the Pope to a place of safety
(Saumur), and they came here on foot.

Some Mamelukes of Buonaparte's
body-guard have deserted from him,
and come in here. We hear that a great
part of Soult's army is already arrived
at Paris. I believe we really shall meet
the great lord.[6] I am just going to hear
mass at the Emperor Alexander's, and
will finish this by-and-by.

[6] Wellington.

Since writing this we have had accounts from Blücher. I fear some of his corps have been roughly handled, and we have lost some cannon and a good many men. The headquarters will move to-morrow to Pont-sur-Seine. I shall stay a day longer before I go to Châtillon. Count d'Escars, who came with Monsieur,[7] arrived here this morning ; Monsieur is stopped at Basle, *et pourquoi?*

What a winter you have had in England! It has been equally severe here since Christmas, but the last week we have had delightful weather, just like May.

Lady Burghersh to her Father

Troyes : February 13

My dearest Papa,—A thousand thanks for your long letter. I was very much

[7] Charles X.

pleased to hear your opinion on the great question, as that opinion is in most cases the soundest I know of, and all you say appears so very just. I wish here there was a little more consistency one way or another, for it is impossible to know (and I am sure many of them do not know themselves) what they mean or wish to do. I do not know if I shall reap any other benefit from my expedition, but I am sure I have matter for astonishment for the rest of my life ; to think how everything has gone on in this most extraordinary war, and been crowned with such complete success, when to all appearance the difference of opinion, the number of cooks, and the uncertainty and inconsistency which goes on in these headquarters should mar the whole business. The whole system is so curious that it must be seen to be believed. Nothing can be

more inconsistent than their present conduct.   When the desire and *but* of all the
Allied Powers seem to be the annihilation
of Buonaparte and his dynasty, each of
them sends a Minister to treat with his
Ministers, and that alone, one should think,
would frighten many from rising against
Buonaparte.   Then, though they appear
all, or nearly all, to agree in the wish of
getting rid of Buonaparte, no two agree in
the choice of who they should put in his
place, but each Power has its own view
and object.   The Emperor Alexander has
set his heart upon entering Paris, and is
exactly like an eager child about it, swearing to the right and left that he does not
mind what they are doing at Châtillon,
that he won't sign peace or think of it till
they are at Paris (Rasumoffsky treating
with Caulaincourt all the time).   Schwarzenberg entreats his Majesty to *raisonner*

un peu ; but his Majesty takes *le mors aux dents*, and sets off from Langres with his guards to push on to the utmost. The rest, finding he will go his own way, are obliged to follow him.

Old Blücher is determined on his side to get to Paris first, and, being used to victory, sets off likewise, pushes on *à tort et à travers*, and consequently gets a fillip, which obliges them now to look about a little. Poor Prince Schwarzenberg has really a hard task to play, as he bears all the responsibility, and yet really cannot act upon his own plans when so many interfere. The Emperor Francis is unhappy for his daughter, and wished to end it all at Basle. Metternich is jealous of the Emperor of Russia, and all and each work with their views, yet to all appearance they are all the best possible friends. The King of Prussia is very quiet ; they say he wishes for more coolness and consistency, but considers himself bound to Alexander, and always remains with him.

We are all curious to see what effect the Bourbons will produce; I fear not much. The people appear too completely debased for one spark of national pride or patriotism to rise from them; they are reduced to abject misery. They all hate and abuse Buonaparte, but none seem to be at all ready to make an effort to better themselves, or to have a recollection of the Bourbon family. If one wishes to abhor a man who has caused such misery as Buonaparte, it is not in the countries that he has carried war into, but in his own empire one must behold it. This was formerly one of the richest and most flourishing commercial towns in France. Now commerce is ruined, and the inhabitants (almost all old men and women) are

all in the most abject distress. There is
one thing which will, I fear, very much
injure the good cause, and that is the
horrid excesses committed by the troops.
Notwithstanding the great pains and very
strict orders of all the commanders, they
cannot keep up discipline, and, if it goes
on, it is impossible to suppose, if the
people have a spark of energy in them,
that they will not attempt to revenge
themselves. The discipline was very well
kept up till we got to Langres, and the
troops everywhere received as friends and
deliverers, but at Langres they met with
the first resistance, a few shots having
been fired in the street, and from that
time there has been no possibility of re-
straining them. It is to the honour of the
Russian and Prussian troops that no com-
plaints have been made of them. The
Cossacks steal and pillage everything, but

that is their *métier*; but the Bavarians
and Würtembergers (who have been
brought up in the French school), and I
am sorry to say some of the Austrians,
have done horrors. All this reconciles me
to going to Châtillon for the present
moment, for I am quite sick of seeing and
hearing of so much misery.

There has been a grand conference
to-day at Prince Metternich's, and, from
what I hear to-night, I believe they think
an armistice likely. Monsieur is at Basle.
Why he remains there, and why he loses
his time when it is so precious, no one
can tell. Providence, who has certainly
blessed this extraordinary warfare with
success up to the present moment, will, I
hope, lead it to the end.

I have written a great deal—of non-
sense I fear—more than you will have
patience to get through, but I should like

to give you some idea of how the great people go on here. I can go by no opinion but my own, for every opinion is different, and so few candid ones can be got at, that one is little the wiser for hearing any of them. If the war continues you must put your plan in execution in the summer, and form your own opinion. I need not say how delightful it would be to me, or half the happiness I should feel, to see you here, but I am sure it is a scene which for a short time would interest and amuse you. . . .

We are all anxiety for news from Lord Wellington since hearing that Soult has withdrawn.[8] . . . The Grand Duchess Catherine talks of taking a journey to England. If she goes there you will see a very clever and delightful person.

[8] From Spain.

N

Lady Burghersh to her Mother

Châtillon-sur-Seine : February 17, 1814

. . . This seems a clean, good town, but I have not been out, for the cold weather is returned with all its rawness, and I have had (for the first time since November) a slight cold. . . .

I left Troyes yesterday morning, and none of the roads in Germany surpassed in badness those to this place. I really never was so jolted. I am extremely well lodged here, which I have not been before for long, and if I could enjoy anything without my better half I should enjoy the cessation from the sight and noise of troops, artillery, wounded, prisoners, and all the horrors of war, which I never can get used to.

The plenipotentiaries [9] spend their

[9] At the Conference then sitting at Châtillon.

lives in giving great dinners to each other, and gorge so effectually that two or three have fallen ill from the effects of their intemperance. It is certainly a luxury to get as much and what one likes to eat, which is not the case in the midst of an immense army quartered in a poor country. Even in 'la bonne Ville de Troyes' it was impossible to get eggs or milk, all the cows having been killed for their flesh. I can drink my tea very well without milk, but I found it a great luxury here this morning, and, greater still, sweet bread. I wrote you a long letter from Troyes and one to papa, but I doubt whether you will get them sooner than this, as I believe the courier was delayed. We had then just heard of the rub which Sacken's corps, under Blücher, had received. Since then there has been some severe and disastrous work in that quarter,

which has given a lesson to the rash im-
prudence of some and the vacillations of
others, and cost a severe loss, but still I
hope we are strong enough to repair it ;
but we were all in a great quandary at
Troyes when the news arrived, and before
we knew how far Blücher would retreat
or Buonaparte pursue. I have just heard
from B., proceeding from Nogent to Bray.
Here things are taking at least a more
consistent turn, and probably to-morrow
may decide a great deal. I am still of the
same opinion as when I was at Basle, that
peace will be made, and the Bourbons left
to shift for themselves, or the French
people to do for themselves what others
will not do for them, but that I fear they
have not energy enough for.

I am to meet all the negotiators the
day after to-morrow at a great dinner,
given (as it is his turn) by C. Stewart,

and if I dine there I shall probably be
obliged to go through with all the others.
Though I am curious to see Caulaincourt,
I had rather avoid the dinners by myself, but B. says that is foolish, and that
I had better see all the fun I can. . . .
I am just out of my wits with delight
at Lord Byron's new book, 'The Corsair.' C. Stewart has got it and lent it
to me.

.   .   .   .   .   -

Lady Burghersh to her Mother

Châtillon-sur-Seine : February 19, 1814

. . . I met Caulaincourt and all the
other plenipotentiaries at dinner yesterday,
and thus satisfied a very great curiosity I
had to see a man of whom I had heard so
much. I can only say, of all the foreigners I have seen, he has by far the best

manners, is the most perfect gentleman, and the most prepossessing address— how vulgar! but I can't find other words. In person he is like Lord Petersham, with a touch of the Duke of Richmond, that is, his sort of very amiable smile, only he looks much younger ; besides which he has an air of the Emperor Alexander, which he takes care to improve by imitating the cut of his hair, &c.   I sat by him at dinner, and could not but admire the tact he showed in his very difficult position amongst us all, when a thousand subjects were to be avoided, and when a man of less tact would appear either too proud or too dejected.   Then he has all the civility and *prévenance* of a Frenchman, without any of their insolence and forwardness. I never saw a countenance so expressive of kindness, sweetness, and openness, and then one recollects the taking of the Duc

d'Enghien ! [1]—so much for outward appearance ! I happened to say at dinner that I
was fond of perfumes, and after dinner he
told me, in the most obliging way, he would
despatch a courier to Paris with orders to
bring back the best perfumes for me, and
begged if there was anything I wished for
from Paris, I would tell him and I should
receive it in two days. This I refused,
as I do not choose voluntarily to put myself under any obligations to the Duc de
Vicenza.[2]

As I expected, if I appeared at one
dinner I should be asked to go to all,
so Rasumoffsky, the plenipotentiary for
Russia, entreated me to dine with him to-
day. I told him that, in the absence of

---

[1] Murdered at Vincennes by Napoleon's order.
Caulaincourt had been sent to demand his extradition
from the Grand Duchy of Baden, but was not really
implicated in the murder.

[2] Title conferred on Caulaincourt by Napoleon.

Lord B., I should not choose to go to
Caulaincourt, and, as I could not refuse
him if I went to others, I had made a rule
to go only to the houses of the English.
He took it perfectly, and wrote me this
morning *le billet le plus aimable* about it,
and I think I managed very well, for I do
not think it would be *convenable* for me
alone to go to the house of any foreigner.
. . . I have now dined with Lord Aberdeen and C. Stewart, and shall probably
with Lord Castlereagh and Lord Cathcart,
and that is all very well amongst my own
compatriotes. But I have sanguine hopes
of seeing B. here to-morrow. The headquarters have returned to Troyes, which
is only three or four hours' ride from here,
and B. has promised to come here to-
morrow. I don't know what they mean
to do, but I know that Buonaparte is em-
ploying all his energy, all his activity, and

all his power, and that we are dilatory, uncertain, and (*entre nous*) frightened— Alexander as much so as any, with all his bravado! But Providence orders it all, I am sure, or we should not be here!

I quite delight in ' Cas.' [3] I had no idea he had so much fun in him, though he is impenetrably cold! . . . I have, while writing this, received yours of the 7th. . . . I am so grieved to think you should worry yourselves about me, and it is exactly what I feared would be when the campaign began. I wish you knew me safe and quiet here. Oh! the relief to one's ears and heart, getting away from the actual scene of war, though one suffers equally in another way from solitude, absence, and anxiety.

I must end—good night, dearest. I wish I could kiss you all round, instead of

[3] Lord Castlereagh.

leaving a solitary room with no one to kiss !

.   .   .   .   .   .

Some letters have been lost, the next one being dated

Lady Burghersh to her Father

Châtillon : March 3, 1814

You will have got the account of the battle last Sunday at Bar-sur-Aube. . . . As we none of us here expected a battle then or there, I was saved a great deal of anxiety in knowing nothing about it till all was over. Poor Burghersh has endured a terrible worry about me during the days when the Austrians abandoned this town, and left us to the French. I wrote Mama word that we could have no communication with the army, as the French were in possession of the roads leading to this town, and were in force at Bar-sur-Seine, six leagues off. Burghersh was therefore quite ignorant of my fate, not knowing whether I should be protected, as I could not pass for a member of the Congress. He therefore gave me up for being taken prisoner, and remained with this idea three days! Meanwhile, I was very safe here; Monsieur Caulaincourt, quite hurt at Lord Aberdeen's thinking Miladi could want protection amongst Frenchmen, and the French troops (except a few dragoons) never having been within the town.

Yesterday General Gyulai and the Prince Royal of Würtemberg, having driven them from Bar-sur-Seine, the Austrian general returned here, and we are all quiet again. Sir C. Stewart is this instant returned from the Emperor's headquarters at Chaumont, where he went the day before yesterday on a visit, and fell in there with Burghersh, who came from Schwarzenberg's headquarters at Colombey for the same purpose. The commissioners are still at Lusigny, treating for an armistice of fifteen days. The French are to send in their final answer to-morrow evening by eight o'clock. Meantime Blücher, who has now a magnificent army (being joined by that of the North), and having got in Buonaparte's rear, is proceeding by Meaux towards Paris, and Buonaparte is turning all his strength upon him, and following him. Our troops, therefore (I mean Schwarzenberg), this day re-enter Troyes, and there I believe they must stop a few days for their pontoons, which on their first alarm they sent back to Langres. A little vigour and firmness may now do a great deal. The Russians have got a report which we don't have, that ' Lord Wellington has begun the campaign most vigorously.' I hope it is true, for it would do us more good than anything. It is certainly, by all accounts, entirely to the obstinate fighting of the cavalry, lately withdrawn from Spain, that Buonaparte owes his late successes ; but I hope they are his last. I am very happy that Prince Schwarzenberg's wound is as trifling as possible — only a spent ball which hit his arm. It is supposed to have been fired by a peasant concealed in a vineyard. Here the plenipotentiaries go on eating and drinking, and entertaining each other, and doing nothing ; but they have now tied Caulaincourt down to the 10th of this month, on which day he is to give his yes or no. My *coup de vent* has left me, and I am perfectly well.

I am lucky here to find myself quartered in the house of a most respectable and good family of the *ancienne noblesse*, furious royalists, and sighing for the Bourbons. There are two sisters, one a widow, with a grown-up son and daughter, who are very agreeable and very amiable people ; and they are as kind to me and as attentive to me as if I belonged to them, which is a great comfort to me, having been so long alone. B. gives me hopes of riding over to me in a day or two. . . .

Pray tell dear Emily I hope to get something for her birthday. . . . It will be the first birthday of hers or mine which we ever spent separated or away from home, and it will seem very very hard to me.

Lady Burghersh to her Father

Châtillon : March 13, 1814

My dearest Papa, — I wrote you yesterday three sheets of paper, but to-day I have taken fright, as the courier goes by Paris, and I spoke openly of things and people, and therefore I have put my three sheets in the fire. You will not be much worse for the loss, but I am too happy to think my letters can afford you a moment's interest or amusement, and that idea is far more likely to make me vain than all the fine things you tell me are said of me ; I am already vain enough, however, to think they will not make me so.

As B. promised (unless some wonderful fit of activity seized our chiefs) that he would come here to-day for my birthday,

I rode out this morning on the Troyes road and met him, and he thinks he can stay two days with me. The heavy machine seems at last to think such a thing as moving from Troyes possible, and some of the troops are already advancing ! Schwarzenberg having contented himself at that place while the whole of the enemy's force was turned upon Blücher, who seems, by common consent, to have the whole game given up to him ! It is too incomprehensible ! They are not in clover either at Troyes, where the want of food is so dreadful that B. says the people literally share with the dogs the dead horses in the streets. The conduct of the troops is shocking, and latterly has become horrible in every degree of pillage, plunder, and cruelty, which of course makes us enemies all over the country, and gives more partisans to Napoleon than all his own powers could do. Here we are anxiously awaiting the decision we expected on the 10th, but on that day Caulaincourt's answer was so far from categorical that it entailed a little more delay, which, however, cannot last above twenty-four hours longer.

There seems (at least, as far as such a head as mine can judge from what one can learn of their different conferences) to be very little chance of peace now, and I expect the Congress will break up in a day or two, when I shall go to the Emperor's headquarters, now at Chaumont, as I cannot be at Schwarzenberg's.

For my own individual feelings nothing can be more disappointing than the idea of a continuance of war and of my existence of the last five months, which it requires some courage to look

o

forward to, for an indefinite period ; for when one takes in anxiety of mind, bodily inconveniences, and the horrid scenes of misery constantly before one's eyes, it cannot be too soon over.   We stand so very differently now (God knows why) from what we did two months ago, that I am not sure a peace now here would not save us from a disgraceful end : but I am getting as bad as my three sheets. . . .

.   .   .   .   .   .

Pray, are the newspapers correct in their opinion of Mr. Kean ?[4]   Is he such a wonderful talent ? . . .

.   .   .   .   .   .

[4] C. Kean, the actor, then first becoming known on the stage in London.

Lady Burghersh to her Sister

Châtillon: March 19, 1814

. . . I wish you would order me a summer riding-habit. . . . You know I like a very short waist behind, and I think the sleeves look better put in with a very few very small plaits on the shoulders. . . . I should wish it light French grey . . . and a man's riding hat of 'shepherd's straw!' . . . The King of Prussia is *le meilleur enfant du monde,* but so very very shy that it is quite ridiculous. As to the Emperor of Austria, he is a complete cipher, guided entirely by Metternich. . . .

The last few days we have had quite hot weather. I suppose where there are trees they are beginning to come out ; but there never was such a bare country as this. In all my rides on different sides of the town, I have never seen a twig, except a row of poplars planted by the side of a beautiful clear fountain, close to the town, where the women carry all the linen to wash. It is very pretty to see them kneeling all along the banks. I go there every day before dinner to pick watercresses. You can't think how kind old Lord Cathcart was! Hearing it was my birthday (when we dined there, when B. was here), he prepared a surprise for me—that is, got a troop of comedians to come to his house, and after dinner had two little pieces performed. The actors were bad, but French people have all a sort of fun and intelligence that makes everything go off well.

Lady Burghersh to her Mother

Châtillon: March 20, 1814

The negotiations ended yesterday, and the Congress is broken up, so there is an end to all my fondest hopes of a quick return home, for I cannot look forwards to a speedy termination by the sword, seeing the same weakness, inconsistency, and timidity prevail amongst us. However, the final breaking up of the negotiations may inspire us with a little more energy, and may make Buonaparte more moderate, seeing the allies will not make peace upon his terms.

Schwarzenberg, after taking a grand determination, and advancing as far as Arcis, one should imagine with the intention of seeing the enemy, upon hearing of him at some distance, orders a retreat, which, on the persuasion of Alexander, incited by Pozzo, was recalled, and returns this day to Bar-sur-Aube.

The Emperors and Kings all fixed their headquarters yesterday at Bar-sur-Seine, which suits me very well, as it is only a few leagues from here, and while they are there I am much better here in my quiet house, with my good people, than if I was amongst them. They say the Emperor of Austria will come here; so much the better if he does, for I shall be very sorry to move from here. . . .

It is a very extraordinary circumstance that nothing is known of Blücher since the 12th, eight days ago. We are in the greatest possible anxiety to hear what direction Lord Wellington has taken. If he should judge it most expedient to turn to La Vendée, &c., which they say is certainly rising, it will be a great disappointment here, for we have all looked to his coming this way. The Ambassadors are all taking their flight. C. Stewart went this morning ; Lord Aberdeen remains here ; Caulaincourt is not yet gone. He was very much *attendri*, I am told, at taking leave of them all yesterday at the last Conference. I am very anxious to hear what line the Emperors intend taking. It seems impossible they should continue the war in this country, which is completely and utterly ruined, devastated, and pillaged. It is a very anxious moment, but I should not think it unlikely that Buonaparte, finding we have been sturdy here, should offer new propositions to the Sovereigns themselves, and I am sure they had better take them if they cannot find abler heads to manage their armies. . . . The brother marshals recriminate terribly upon each other, but there is, I am afraid, little doubt that our good friend deserves it more than old Vorwärts.[5] . . .

.   .   .   .   .   .

. . . The ladies of this house, having offered me a safe opportunity by a friend of theirs in Paris, I wrote a letter to Edward Paget. I despair of getting an answer, but I thought he would like to hear news of his family. . . .

Lady Burghersh to her Mother

Châtillon: March 21

. . . Schwarzenberg has thought better of his plan of retreat, and remains with his whole army assembled at Arcis, a very fine position. The enemy is at Plancy, on the other side of the river. This being the case, we expect some event hourly. The Em-

---

[5] Blücher's nickname.

perors are all gone from Bar-sur-Seine to
Bar-sur-Aube. Lord Aberdeen, Stadion,
and Rasumoffsky remain here until something is known which will decide whether
we are to move backwards or forwards. I
shall remain with them, and move with
them. I hope very shortly to be able
to rejoin B., for this long separation is
dreadful. I should think next move might
enable me to be with him. Caulaincourt
left this, this morning. All the rest of the
negotiators, except the three I have named,
went yesterday. The Austrian garrison
remains here, and Maurice Liechtenstein's
corps covers us. If things go well, I
hope we may return to Troyes. If we
get a check, or are frightened, we shall
go to Chaumont. We have no news of
Blücher. . . .

I have been buying horses, for there
are no more post horses left in the coun-

try, and laying in stores of provisions in case of moving into the sacked towns or villages.

Lady Burghersh to her Mother

Dijon: March 26, 1814

. . . I must give you some details as to my affairs, and how I come to be here when B. is, alas! so far away. This comes of following the wise heads of diplomatists. When I wrote to you last from Châtillon we were all in uncertainty what we were to do, but upon Tuesday last it was decided that we should go to Chaumont (supposing the Emperor at Bar-sur-Aube), and we accordingly set off on Wednesday morning in a train of twelve carriages, with an escort of hussars and Cossacks. Arrived at Chaumont, we found the tocsin ringing, and the whole town in an uproar

of alarm and confusion, and they told us a
corps of 16,000 French were within four
or five leagues of the town, and a body of
2,000 armed and organised peasants close
to it. Upon this it was necessary to de-
camp, and without even waiting to bait
our horses, away we went in the direction
of Langres. At about three leagues
from Chaumont we found 2,000 Austrians
bivouacked, and here it was determined to
pass the night and wait the result of the
morning to know if the French corps
entered Chaumont or went off the other
way, and also to know where the Emperor
was, which no one knew, but it was said
he had gone to Brienne.

Luckily it was a fine night, and I
think a bivouac by no means unpleasant,
it is such a very curious sight ; but only
conceive poor me sitting at a great fire, in
the open air, in the middle of the night,

surrounded by soldiers and horses! At
about two in the morning, however, I got
into the carriage, though I could not sleep,
the scene was so curious.   At daylight
we got intelligence that the Emperor was
gone to Dijon, and desired all the diplomatists to follow him.   I never was so
thunderstruck at any news, but there was
no help for it.   We went on that day to
Langres, where we stopped the night, and
arrived here yesterday, our horses quite
done up, myself not at all so.   I am as
strong as Hercules!   But here I find
myself as much out of the reach of the
armies as if I was in America, and even
our communications are cut off, the French
being at Bar-sur-Aube, *between* us and
them, but meantime it is a most painful
situation to bear, and an anxiety almost
too great.   Conceive, it is now seven days
since I knew anything at all of B., and he

is still worse off, for he has not heard of me since I left Châtillon, and therefore cannot know if I am here or not. Perhaps no one ever got (for the time it lasts) a heavier load of anxiety to bear, but I have learnt lately to bear a great deal.

. . . It is quite a pity I am not at ease and happy enough to enjoy this town. It is quite beautiful, and the only town I have yet been in where the shops are all open, and full, and looking gay. They say the theatre is excellent, but I cannot go while in this terrible state of anxiety and suspense. I walk about all day, and am followed and stared at like a wild beast. You would be amused at the remarks which I hear made out loud.

You never saw such a *beauty* as Lord Castlereagh has become. He is as brown as a berry, with a fine bronzed colour, and wears a fur cap with gold,

and is really quite *charming*. There
never was anybody so looked up to as he
is here.

.   .   .   .   .   .

Can you conceive anything more vexa-
tious for me, who hoped by getting to the
Emperor's headquarters soon to rejoin B.,
and the last they know was of the junction
of Schwarzenberg's and Blücher's armies,
and the headquarters being at Chalons,
and me down at Dijon! It is impossible
to conceive what can have possessed old
Francis to come here.   Lord Castlereagh
is here, all the civil characters, and Lord
Bradford is also here, and very kind and
friendly to me ; but I never before was so
uncomfortable and uneasy, or in such a
dreadful predicament.   I hope it won't
last long, and that I may soon be able to
get away.   Meanwhile I am excellently
lodged with very obliging people, and this

is much the best town I have been in since Frankfurt. . . .

A thousand thanks for the tea. I thought it such a luxury this morning, for I had been drinking the horrid stuff they sell in France at a louis a pound! I went (as usual) this morning poking into the shops here, and bought a gown for you, but I cannot send it by this conveyance

.   .   .   .   .   .

Sunday, March 27

I continue this morning, being just returned from Mass in a very fine old church here. You cannot think what a nice town this is, and there is an air of comfort and ease which I have not seen before in France. Certainly, if my mind could be easy, I am most extremely lucky to find myself here, where I enjoy (with security) repose and a cessation of the horrid sights of war; but I fear, finding themselves so well off here, the Court will stick.

All one can hope is that the union of Blücher and Schwarzenberg will produce a grand *coup*, and finish the business. We have Maurice Liechtenstein's army here.

I find this morning I can squeeze your gown into a letter, so I send it. I am afraid you will think the stripes too large, but it is the rage now in France to have everything enormous, and this is the smallest pattern I could get. Never was anything so frightful as the French fashions—everything *outré* to a degree of monstrosity. The hats get worse and worse; they make them now with very narrow, small pokes, and crowns two feet high, and the front covered with enormous bows and bunches of flowers—and these are worn by every creature.

I am so stared at in my cottage bonnet that I really don't know what to do, for I cannot put one of these horrors on my head ! . . .

I hope you will soon make acquaintance with the Grand Duchess Catherine, and be as much pleased with her as I was. She was so kind to me. The Emperor Alexander's two young brothers, the Grand Dukes Nicholas and Michael, are coming to the army ; they are sixteen and eighteen years old. They say the eldest (Nicholas[6]) is quite beautiful.

Tuesday, 29th

I add a line to tell you the Emperor has just received the news of a great

[6] The Emperor Nicholas, who died in 1855, during the Crimean war.

victory gained by Schwarzenberg, at Fère
Champenoise on the 25th, in which he
took 8,000 prisoners and sixty cannon.
We don't know particulars yet, or whether
Blücher shared or not. Buonaparte himself is at Vaudœuvre, so our communication is still cut off, but this must drive him
very soon off.

I am sure you and Mama will have felt
a great deal for poor Lord March.[7] I trust
he is doing well, though I was grieved at
the account Gurwood (from whom I got a
letter to-day) gives of him. How does the
poor Duke bear it ? I am very anxious to
hear particulars of Arthur's slight wound.[8]
Gurwood says the ball went an inch into
his thigh. It makes me shudder! We
have got this morning an account of the
proceedings at Bordeaux ; there never was

[7] Wounded in Spain.
[8] At the Battle of Orthez, February 27, 1814.

anything so good, and we are all in hopes the good example may be followed here, and the white cockade mounted.

This part of the country has not as yet suffered from the bad conduct of the troops—as yet all has been kept in good order and discipline.

We are still cut off from intelligence from *our* army, though we hope it will soon be free, for Buonaparte certainly cannot stay long on his present line.

.   .   .   *.*   .   .

Lady Burghersh to her Mother

Dijon: April 4

At last, my dearest Mama, I am relieved from the dreadful suspense and anxiety I have endured for thirteen days, and I have just received a letter from B., dated Paris! April 1st.   There is no describing my sensations at seeing this *blessed* letter after such an age of anxious expectation, having heard nothing since I left Châtillon, excepting of the battle fought at Fère Champenoise, of which I had just heard when I wrote my last letter, but we knew only the fact of there having been a battle and a victory on our side, and you may believe what I felt in my heart at hearing nothing more. Poor B. was in equal distress, not having heard from me, and not having a guess where I was gone to, with the knowledge of Chaumont, &c., having been in danger. All this prevented him from enjoying the entry into Paris, which seems to have been the most magnificent and most extraordinary event in the annals of the world, perhaps. You will have the details in the despatches ; at this moment we are all perfectly *mad* here, and I doubt much if I can write one word of sense with all the feelings that work me, but I know the only thing I can do is to sit down and write to you.   To be sure, it is enraging, after going through so much, not to be 'in at the death,' and I have missed entering Paris with the victors, but I must console myself with many others in the same predicament with the knowledge of the total impossibility of our doing so, as Buonaparte contrived so cleverly to cut us off.   For with all my grumblings in my last letters, we did not run here a moment too soon.   Buonaparte slept at Bar-sur-Aube in the very bed the Emperor Francis had left that same morning, and the French troops passed through Chaumont and came to the stop where we bivouacked the day after we were there.

I feel so grateful and so happy, after all the dangers we have both been in, to know that it is over, that I have really heard from him (which I began to think impossible), that he is well and safe, and that we may hope soon to be together. I don't yet know the Emperor's plans, and I don't much think I can well leave this place till he does, but I suppose I shall see Metternich to-night, and I hope in a very few days we may all meet in Paris. B. writes to me on the 1st, expecting to leave Paris the next day, to collect and go after what remnant Buonaparte can have with him in the direction of Sens; but that will, I hope, be short and easy work.

Poor Rapatel, General Moreau's aide-de-camp, was killed in the battle before Paris. I am very sorry for him. His letter to Madame Moreau, published in the English papers last September, made him interesting, and I have seen him often at headquarters, and liked him much. The last time he dined with us at Troyes he told me he meant to go directly to England to Madame Moreau, and it must be a great blow to her, poor soul; it was said she would marry him. Colonel Campbell, a Scotchman attached to Lord Cathcart, was severely wounded in the same battle by a Cossack, who took him for a Frenchman. I have not heard of anyone else whom I know. Neither Lord Cathcart's nor C. Stewart's despatches are arrived, so there is only B.'s (which I think an incomparable one) which has been translated into French and stuck up all over the town with the Emperor Alexander's declaration, and now all the people are walking about in white cockades. What do you say to Talleyrand being the first person to mount the white cockade in Paris !

Maria Louisa left Paris for Rambouillet on the 29th. It really appears like a dream, all of it, after the gloomy prospects we had a month ago; but, as Alexander told me, '*c'est le bon Dieu qui guide nos armées*,' and I am sure that is true. I long to return to the army to see how 'cocky' all the Russians will be; they are excellent fun when they have performed any *feat !*

I meant to write to dear Emily by this courier, but I cannot; but my first letter from Paris shall be to her, and I must put into this letter all I wanted to tell her. First, Count Weissenberg (to whom Lord Westmorland gave a letter of Emily's to me, and the spy-glass) was taken prisoner on his journey, and carried before Buonaparte at Bar-sur-Aube. He had the most extraordinary conversation with him upon the state of affairs, in which Buonaparte owned to him that his own situation was desperate, but said the Bourbons had no chance, '*car ils sont devenus étrangers à la France.*' After taking everything from

him, even his clothes, they set Weissenberg at liberty, and he came on here. He
contrived, just as he was taken, to burn all
his letters and papers, so Emily need not
fear the *Moniteur,* but I lose her letter. . . .

This evening the town is illuminated,
and all the people walking about with
white cockades and *flambeaux,* calling out
' *Vive le Roi !* ' One is really beside oneself, and I think I am displaying no little
prudence and moderation in staying here
one instant, and not setting off this instant
to join *my own headquarters.* Conceive
how fine it must have been to see Alexander enter Paris at the head of his
beautiful guards (20,000), attended by the
King of Prussia at the head of *his* guards
(7,000), and Schwarzenberg and Blücher
together. I can just fancy Alexander in
all his glory ! He was to go to the opera
the day after (the 2nd). B. was lodged in

a palace in the Rue 'de la Concorde.' He
had not been to any *sight*, and, indeed, his
uneasiness about me prevents his giving
me as many details as I still hope to have.
We expect another courier to-night or to-
morrow morning. Schwarzenberg's aide-
de-camp, Szechenyi,[9] brought the account
to-day. I have not seen him yet, but I
suppose I shall when he has done with
the Emperor and Ministers. . . .

Tuesday night

I am just returned from the theatre,
where I have been chaperoned by Lord
Castlereagh and all the English. It has
been a most interesting evening, the theatre
crammed quite full, and everybody in white
cockades. They gave ' Richard Cœur de
Lion,' and every part at all applicable to

---

[9] Count Stephan Szechenyi, a Hungarian statesman,
well known in later years.

the present situation was caught up by the
audience and produced shouts of ' *Vive
Louis XVIII.! Vive les Bourbons!*' Before the curtain drew up they called for a
song out of the ' Déserteur,' with a refrain
of ' *Vive le Roi!*' which was joined in with
the greatest enthusiasm. Between the acts
the curtain drew up and discovered a
placard with ' *Vive les Alliés!*' under a
fleur-de-lys, and one of the actors came on
and sang an incomparable parody on that
very beautiful romance, ' Oh Richard, oh
mon Roi!' I cannot describe to you the
effect of the beginning, '*Oh Louis, oh mon
Roi!*' or the violent enthusiasm with which
it was received, everybody getting up and
waving white handkerchiefs, &c. Nothing
could be more affecting. The parody went
on, ' *Oh Louis, oh mon Roi! tout l'univers
avec moi s'intéresse à ta personne.*'

In the midst of this exulting moment I

cannot help feeling for poor Maria Louisa, who by every account is certainly sincerely in love with Buonaparte, and what a dreadful situation she is in! The poor Emperor Francis shows just the feeling a good father must show for her, knowing her sacrifice to be inevitable. It is supposed she is gone from Rambouillet to Orleans.

Alexander did not occupy the Tuileries, but lodged in Talleyrand's house.

The next letter (or letters) of the series is not forthcoming, but in later years Lady Burghersh used often to tell the story of her journey from Dijon to Paris, and embodied her recollections in a memorandum.

Though she boasts in her letter of her prudence and moderation in not setting off at once from Dijon to join her husband, that prudence did not last long. However,

when she spoke of starting to Prince
Metternich, Lord Castlereagh, and Lord
Aberdeen (the three advisers her husband
had desired her to consult in any emer-
gency), they all told her that, in consequence
of the reports brought by Szechenyi and
the couriers who succeeded him of the
state of the country, it would be utterly
impossible to think of moving from Dijon
till the roads were restored, safe conducts
organised, escorts provided, &c., and that
the Emperor Francis himself would not
be able to start for a week or ten days at
least. It occurred to her, however, that
although all these delays and precautions
might be necessary for these great official
personages, she could do very well by
herself, so, without saying anything more,
she packed her carriage, got horses, and
set off with her maid and servant. She
never experienced any real difficulty, but
by civility and paying well managed to get
on perfectly, with the exception of one
little fright, when she fell in with some

French soldiers, who insisted on taking her prisoner and carrying her into the next town to be examined. Fortunately their commander was a good-natured man, and on her representing to him that it could do no one any good to detain or hinder a poor unprotected woman like herself, only wanting to '*rejoindre mon mari*,' he at first made a show of detaining her, but soon saying, '*Ah, ça, Madame, vous seriez bien contente si je vous laissais continuer votre route, n'est-ce pas?*' he let her go on her way, and this was the only real difficulty she had.

After travelling three days and nights. she got in the evening after dark to the gates of Paris, which were guarded by sentinels of the allied armies. She inquired her way to Lord Burghersh's quarters, where she found all his servants, but he himself had gone out to dinner. She went up into his room, and was especially delighted to find on his table the miniature of herself which he always carried about

with him. He came home a short time
afterwards, and could scarcely believe his
eyes, when, on turning to the courtyard of
the house, he recognised her carriage un-
packing, for the idea of her accomplishing
the journey from Dijon in this way, before it
was possible for anyone else to come, had
never entered his mind! He rushed up-
stairs, and the delight of the meeting in such
different circumstances may be imagined.

The great people at Dijon waiting for
their escorts did not get up to Paris for
several days ; they were exceedingly an-
noyed when they found they had been
distanced, and the journey they were
all afraid of safely accomplished by a
young unprotected woman, and she used
afterwards to say that Lord Castlereagh
and Lord Aberdeen had never quite for-
given her, but were always sore when any
allusion was made to her getting to Paris
before them.

The following is the first letter from
Paris which has been preserved :—

Lady Burghersh to ——

I am in the greatest rage that ever was to-night! Only conceive, just as I was beginning to enjoy myself, and be quite happy here, thinking all my lonely hours at an end for ever, Burghersh is named to attend Napoleon to the Isle of Elba. He is to be escorted by a Russian (General Schouvaloff), an Austrian (General Koller), and an Englishman (B.). I would go with him with all my heart, but that they will not allow, and I suppose, indeed, I could not do so, as they will travel with him, dine with him, &c. It will be just like guarding a wild beast. They set off to-morrow, and are to embark him on the sixth day, so B. will probably be back here in nine days.[1] There never was anything so hard on me; we were so happy here, and this morning only were agreeing that at the end of three weeks— by which time probably the army will be sent into cantonments—we would go back to England. I am more than half tempted to go immediately back to England, but he wishes me to remain here till his return. I do think it is a cruel thing on me, but it is a curious mission to be sent on.

To-day Prince Esterhazy and Prince Wenzel Liechtenstein returned from Fontainebleau, where they had been sent by the Emperor of Austria to Maria Louisa. They dined with us to-day, and gave me an account of her. She cried very much, but consented to leave Buonaparte, for which

[1] On finding he was expected to remain at Elba, Lord B. declined the post, and Colonel Campbell was appointed.

I think she is a monster, for she certainly
pretended love for him, and he always
behaved very well to her. She said she
would not see him before he goes, for
that if she saw him and that he asked her
to come with him, she knew she could not
refuse him ; but that to obey her father,
and for the good of her child, she agreed
to go to Vienna. She showed them the
King of Rome, and they say he is the
most beautiful child they ever saw. She
is to have the Duchy of Parma and Gua-
stalla. I think it is quite disgusting in her
to abandon him in his misfortunes, after
pretending, at least, to idolise him in his
prosperity,[2] and I feel exactly the same

---

[2] Subsequently, in Italy, Lady Burghersh formed a
warm friendship with the Empress Maria Louisa, which
lasted uninterruptedly until the death of Maria Louisa.
She always spoke of her as a most lovable person, affectionate, and generous almost to excess, and possessing
much common sense, which was however marred by her
extreme diffidence and distrust of herself, which made
her always the tool of others. This want of self-reliance

about all his marshals, &c., who have left him.

Yesterday morning Monsieur[3] made his entrance into Paris, and was received with the most violent acclamations. He came in on horseback with a large *cortège*, went through all the principal streets, which were filled with people with white

was the real cause of the acts for which history blames her; her own instincts, had she had the courage to follow them, would have guided her far more rightly. Her own wish was to remain in Paris and place herself and her son under the protection of the Allied Sovereigns, but she yielded to the advice of Joseph Buonaparte, who had been ordered by Napoleon not to let her fall into the hands of the Allies. She wished to follow him to Elba, but gave up this, her undoubted duty, in deference to the opposition of her father, the Emperor Francis, and Prince Metternich, who practised unscrupulously on her fears and credulity, keeping back all Napoleon's letters, and making her believe that he had got a mistress with him, and cared nothing for her. These statements (which were untrue) made her very unhappy, for she was really attached to Napoleon, and often said she had been happy with him, though she was afraid of him, and that he had always been kind to her.

[3] Afterwards Charles X.

cockades, and went immediately to Notre
Dame, to hear the *Te Deum.* I was
there, and it was certainly a magnificent
sight. When he entered the church, every
creature shouted out ' *Vive le Roi !*' '*Vive
Louis,*' &c., and waved handkerchiefs,
clasped hands, &c., with a degree of enthusiasm which I never saw in England
for anything. I never saw anything so
beautiful or so perfect as Monsieur's whole
manner. He was of course very much
affected ; but there was something so
noble, so thoroughbred, so modest, and so
perfectly princely in his look and manner,
that it was really delightful. So different to
the *fanfaronnade* with which Alexander
courts popular adoration. But what I
own disgusted me, was to see Monsieur
surrounded by Talleyrand, Ney, Marmont,
Oudinot, &c., the National Guard, and the
very populace who three weeks ago were

shouting ' *Vive l'Empereur !* ' All I have
seen of the French people, and particularly
the Parisians, makes me think them the
most despicable set of animals, and I do
heartily pity the Bourbons, and all their
ancient followers, to find themselves
amongst these of the new *régime*. How
they are to be governed, or how things
will ever go on between old and new, God
knows ; but all the events of the last
fortnight are so extraordinary, one can
only wonder and wonder on.

As to the town of Paris, the beauty
and magnificence of it surpasses anything
I could form an idea of. All the Arcs de
Triomphe, pillars, &c., which Buonaparte
has erected, are perfect. The Senate have
ordered all emblems of him to be destroyed ; they have already taken down
a colossal statue of him, which was in the
Place Vendôme, and are taking away all

the N's and eagles which are stuck in all
parts of the public buildings.   Monsieur
is lodged in the Tuileries in Maria
Louisa's apartments.

I have not yet been into a single shop.
Monday, I drove about all day to look at
the town—yesterday was spent at Notre
Dame, and to-day I was all the morning
in the Gallery of the Louvre.   It is quite
impossible to give an idea of the beauty of
this gallery, 1,500 feet long and filled with
the finest paintings ; but it would take one
a fortnight, I am sure, spending every day
there, to see it well.   The statues (with
the famous originals of the Apollo, the
Venus and Laocoon) are downstairs. I have
been to the Théâtre Français only, which
in size and shape reminds me of Drury
Lane, but not near so handsome. I meant
to have seen Talma to-night in 'Œdipe,'
but we had a dinner, and they stayed so

late, that when we got there the play was over. I never heard of anything so bad as the society here—not only naughty to an excess, but so vulgar, such *mauvais ton* that I do not think I would spend six months here for a great deal. B. saw a little of it before I came, and he says he could not live with the people who form the society here, it is so shocking. G. is the great person and dear friend of all the first people here, because she was a favourite of the Emperor's ; and Paër, the famous composer, is also received as a great person.

I met Grassini at dinner yesterday at C. Stewart's (who has got the most beautiful house in Paris). She is very handsome, and after dinner she sang quite divinely. Pray tell Mary[4] she remembered her quite well, and said she was '*une*

---

[4] Her eldest sister, Lady Bagot.

charmante personne qui avait milles bontés pour moi.'   She was also at Notre Dame, just behind me.   I was next to the Princess de Benevente, whom you will know better as Madame Talleyrand.   I confess I cannot stomach treating these people *de princes et princesses*, and I cannot conceive how the old French will bear it.   There never was anything like the *tourbillon*, the noise, the constant succession of events here : one's head really turns round with it.

I am most excessively anxious to get home—dear home—even if I had not all of you to return to : there is nothing in Paris, after seeing the sights, that one could, I think, make one's mind up to live with, or for, even for a few weeks.   I think in less than a month I shall certainly be again with you—thank God !

Lady Burghersh to her Mother

Paris : Monday Evening, April 18

My dearest Mama,—As I wrote to Emily and to Papa this morning I have little to add to-night but what fills my mind—the delightful idea of seeing you so soon. I am sure you will be much amused here for a little while, though, if I know your taste, I think a *séjour* in Paris would suit you as little as me ; but you have just seized the right moment to see many extraordinary sights and characters, and I am sure it will answer to Papa. I can hardly believe that I shall so soon have such happiness as to be with you again.

I saw Edward [5] again to-day ; he inquired most tenderly after you, and said

---

[5] Edward Paget, Lord Anglesey's brother, who had been detained for many years as a prisoner in France.

I looked so like you in my carriage this morning that it did him good. I am just come from the Théâtre de l'Odéon, that is, the Italian Opera, where we saw 'Figaro' badly done enough. The house is very pretty. To-morrow we have half a hundred Russians to dine with us. How eager I am for you to arrive, and I think all day long who we will have to meet you, and introduce you to, &c. ! B. is really almost (I won't let him be quite) as delighted as I am at the idea of seeing you. He is looking famously well. Pray try and see the Grand Duchess Catherine before you come. You will see the beauteous Constantine [6] here. The two young brothers are not come yet.

Pray is M. de Gontaut St. Blancard

---

[6] The Grand Duke Constantine of Russia, who was said to be as hideous as his brother, Nicholas, was handsome.

the person I remember as Aimé Gontaut? Such a person called on me to-day while I was out, and I take it to be him. The two Polignacs[7] are both here. Armand dines with us to-morrow.

Lady Burghersh to her Mother

Paris : April 20

. . . I have succeeded with very great difficulty in getting apartments for you, and to-day have engaged some very nice ones quite newly done up, not far from here, though not so near as I could wish, but not five minutes' walk, close to the Place Vendôme, in a good street. They will be ready for you on Sunday, and I

[7] The Polignacs and Gontauts and many other *émigrés* had received much kindness in England from Lady Burghersh's parents and her aunt Mrs. Villiers, who had spent some time in Paris immediately before the Revolution.

have engaged them for a fortnight from that day, and you may keep them on if you like. The price sounds enormous—500 francs for the fortnight—about twenty-five guineas—but it is quite impossible to get anything cheaper. Besides, B. having gone himself about all yesterday, I sent the two A.D.C.'s into every corner, and they could find nothing else likely to suit. You will have linen, china, the use of a kitchen (which, however, you will of course never want), if you like, and I think it will be very comfortable.

Lord Binning [8] says there is a good inn at Montreuil, where you had better sleep the night you leave Calais, and I hear you will also find good inns both at Abbeville and Beauvais, as the distance may suit you. Be careful of the difference between

[8] Who had just arrived—almost the first English tourist—from England.

la poste and *l'auberge*. *La poste* furnishes
nothing but horses ; and if you go to the
auberge for them, you wait hours; but
you must go at once to the *auberge* if
you mean to put up. I am afraid you
will find the best of French inns but bad ;
but they say the three places I have mentioned are as good as you can find in
France, and the roads capital all along. I
am quite panting for your arrival, and I
grudge everything that happens till you
come. I believe I shall die with pleasure
at seeing you again. To-morrow I am
going to spend the day at St. Cloud, where
Schwarzenberg is established, and gives
me a dinner ; the day after we have a
great dinner of half-a-dozen Princes at
home, and I believe Madame Ney will
give a ball, and I grudge it all before you
arrive. We dined to-day at Lord Cathcart's ; old Blücher was there—I was quite

shocked at the alteration in him since his illness. He is quite broken, and I do not think he will live long. He is going soon to England. Pozzo goes to London to-night, but will return soon. I shall hope to hear from you from Calais very soon, and you must let me know how you mean to travel as to speed, that I may know when to expect you. I must say good-night. It is nearly one o'clock, and my eyes draw straws. Heaven bless you. Thank God, this is nearly the last letter you will get from me !

Yr. most aff.,

P.

The letters now cease. Soon after the Wellesley Poles reached Paris, the Duke of Wellington arrived. Lord and Lady Burghersh were walking down the street one day when they saw a travelling carriage coming along, in which they re-

cognised their uncle. He immediately
jumped out and joined them, and was
very soon the object of a great popular
ovation. The whole party remained some
weeks in Paris, through the *fêtes* of the
Restoration, returning to England at the
same time as the Allied Sovereigns paid
their famous visit.

In the autumn of that year Lord Burghersh was appointed Minister at Florence
—exchanging military for diplomatic service. Here they remained (with occa-
sional visits to England) for sixteen years ;
subsequently, after an interval of some
years, they spent nine years in Berlin
and six in Vienna—in the same capacity—
retiring finally in 1856. They were noted
everywhere for their hospitality ; there was
hardly a distinguished person in Europe
whom they did not at some time entertain,
and nothing could well be more brilliant
than their position abroad from a worldly
point of view. Lady Burghersh thoroughly
appreciated the intellectual advantages of

the cultivated and brilliant society she enjoyed, but nevertheless her heart was always in her home. Twelve children were born to her (but of these several died in earliest infancy, and others she lost in the prime of life); they were the engrossing care and interest of her life; in their childhood she tended them and worked for them—herself—never leaving them if she could possibly help it, and never allowing social duties to interfere with her personal care of them. Later in life she reaped the reward of this self-denying affection in the devoted love of her children, who found in her society their greatest delight, and to whom she was ever the most delightful of companions, as well as the wisest of counsellors and friends.

She was—especially through her intimacy with her uncle, the Duke of Wellington (to whom she was as a daughter), and many of the prominent politicians of the day—much mixed up in politics and public affairs, but she never posed as a

' political ' woman or ' leader ' of any kind, holding the now old-fashioned view that a woman's influence is none the less real for being silent and unobtrusive, and she was herself certainly an instance of the combination of the most perfect devotion to domestic duties with wide interests and a powerful mind.

She was left a widow in 1859, and lived on for twenty years in comparative retirement, but happy in the society of her children and grandchildren until her death, at the age of eighty-six, on February 18, 1879.

PRINTED BY

SPOTTISWOODE AND CO., NEW-STREET SQUARE

LONDON

R

MR. MURRAY'S
NEW AND FORTHCOMING WORKS.

————•◦•————

A SKETCH OF THE LIFE OF GEORGIANA LADY
DE ROS. With some Reminiscences of her Family and
Friends, including the Duke of Wellington. By her Daughter
the Hon. Mrs. SWINTON. With Portraits. Crown 8vo. 7s. 6d.
'It is with regret that we take leave of this charming little book—an unaffected
and agreeable record of a gracious and kindly life.'—ST. JAMES'S BUDGET.

THE DIARY OF AN IDLE WOMAN IN CONSTAN-
TINOPLE. By Mrs. MINTO ELLIOT, Author of 'The Diary
of an Idle Woman in Italy,'—'In Sicily,' &c. With Map
and Illustrations. Crown 8vo. 14s.

THE PAMIRS ; being a Narrative of a Year's Expedition
on Horseback and on Foot through Kashmir, Western Tibet,
Chinese Tartary, and Russian Central Asia. By the EARL OF
DUNMORE, F.R.G.S. With Maps and Illustrations. 2 vols.
Crown 8vo. [Shortly.

A MEMOIR OF H.R.H. THE LATE DUKE OF
CLARENCE. Written with the sanction of H.R.H. the
Prince of Wales. By JAMES EDMUND VINCENT. With
Portraits and Illustrations by William Simpson and others.
Crown 8vo. [Shortly.

JENNY LIND THE ARTIST. A New and Abridged
Edition of the Memoir of Madame JENNY LIND-GOLDSCHMIDT,
1820–1851. From MSS. and Documents collected by Mr.
Goldschmidt. By H. SCOTT-HOLLAND, Canon of St. Paul's
Cathedral ; and W. S. ROCKSTRO, Author of 'The Life of
Mendelssohn.' With Portraits. Crown 8vo. [Shortly.

THE LIFE AND CORRESPONDENCE OF ARTHUR
PENRHYN STANLEY, late Dean of Westminster. By
ROWLAND E. PROTHERO, M.A., Barrister-at-Law, late Fellow
of All Souls' College, Oxford ; with the co-operation and
sanction of the Very Rev. G. G. BRADLEY, Dean of Westminster. With Portraits. 2 vols. 8vo. [Shortly.

SCRAMBLES AMONGST THE ALPS IN THE YEARS

1860-69, including the History of the First Ascent of the Matterhorn. By EDWARD WHYMPER. An *Edition de Luxe* (Fourth Edition). With 5 Maps and 136 Illustrations. Price £2. 12s. 6d. net.

This edition is being printed by Messrs. R. & R. Clark, of Edinburgh, on paper specially made for the purpose by Messrs. Dickinson. As it is intended that it shall be the best Edition of this work, and the number printed will be limited, early application should be made to booksellers. · [*Shortly.*

JOURNEYS IN PERSIA AND KURDISTAN ; with a

Summer in the Upper Karun Region, and a visit to the Nestorian Rayahs. By Mrs. BISHOP (ISABELLA BIRD). With Maps and Illustrations. 2 vols. 24s.

SIX MONTHS IN THE SANDWICH ISLANDS,

among the Palm Groves, Coral Reefs, and Volcanoes. By ISABELLA L. BIRD (Mrs. BISHOP). Illustrations. 7s. 6d.

A LADY'S LIFE IN THE ROCKY MOUNTAINS.

By ISABELLA L. BIRD (Mrs. BISHOP). Illustrations. 7s. 6d.

UNBEATEN TRACKS IN JAPAN. Travels in the

Interior of Japan. By ISABELLA L. BIRD (Mrs. BISHOP). Illustrations. 7s. 6d.

LADY DUFFERIN'S JOURNAL OF VICE-REGAL

Life in India: During the Years 1884-88. Illustrations. 7s. 6d.

LADY DUFFERIN'S CANADIAN JOURNAL, 1872-78.

Crown 8vo. 12s.

THE BARONAGE AND THE SENATE ; or, the

House of Lords in the Past, the Present, and the Future. By WM. CHARTERIS MACPHERSON. 8vo. 16s.

CONTENTS:—The Origin and Constitution of the House of Lords. —The Radical Case against the House of Lords.—Radical Remedies.—Conservative Reforms.

'A most sound, interesting, and informing book ; and very few men who have not made a careful study of constitutional history will close it without feeling that they are better informed about the history of the House of Lords, its uses and its position in the constitution, than they were when they began.'—ST. JAMES'S BUDGET.

JOHN MURRAY, Albemarle Street.

www.ingramcontent.com/pod-product-compliance
Lightning Source LLC
Chambersburg PA
CBHW020347030726
47496CB00007B/2036